THE TRUE STORY
OF GABRIEL MICHAEL SANTORUM

ARE WE LIVING IN AN ALTERNATIVE HISTORY?

Albert Ebstein

Note to the readers:
Be careful, this book is magical. It is a time opera. You can read it like a spy
novel between East and West, on a scale of the whole history, or rather of two
parallel histories. As soon as you have started reading, you will not be able to
leave it before the end, because it reveals secrets that no intelligence service
knows yet. Uchrony and conspiracy theory meet in this book. Do not start reading at night, because you risk to lose a night's sleep. Reading it will not leave
you unscathed. It will dismiss the generally accepted ideas and will upset your
most private beliefs.

Table of contents

*"Truth is stranger than fiction,
but it is because Fiction is obliged to stick
to possibilities; Truth isn't."*
(Mark Twain)

STILLBORN

Gabriel Michael Santorum was born in 1996 in the United States. Born extremely premature after only five months of pregnancy, he dies two hours after his birth. Two of his sisters are called Elizabeth and Maria. He is the fourth child of The Republican Senator Richard John Santorum. He could not live in our history, because in the first history the U.S. government put him in charge of rewriting it, therefore of crushing it and erasing himself, in order to save America and freedom. He had never existed, everything had to be forgotten, it was a suicide mission and he knew it.

When Richard and his wife cry over their dead child, they ignore that their youngest son is a national hero who saved America in the True History. They do not even know that there is a True History, which preceded them and almost finished dramatically. They are absorbed in their grief, desperate, and do not understand why God inflicts them this event. Neither do they know that their son is the Gabriel from the Bible and the Quran, and the Michael whose voices Joan of Arc could hear. Their son is an angel adored by half humanity. He has created, as he was ordered, the three religions of the Book, using "miracles" and special effects. He is both Saint Gabriel and Saint Michael, *sanctum sanctorum*, the Saint of Saints! They do not know that in our history he has given his name to Santorini, the volcano in the Aegean Sea whose eruption saved Moses, when he was going to get caught up by Pharaoh's cavalry. Worse, they do not know that their son is the father of John the Baptist and Jesus, whose name he has chosen because it means "Yahweh saves". Yahweh who saves America (*God bless America*), we will see how. The very catholic Senator Santorum does not know that he is Jesus's grandfather!

"History is a lie believed by everybody."
(Napoleon)

"History is written by the winners."
(Brasillach)

THE TRUE HISTORY

Our history is scattered with miracles that historians criticize when they are reported by religions, but curiously not when they are reported by themselves. The religious believe in their miracles, it is an act of faith. The historians "believe" in their own and it is then a blatant lack of critical faculty. In both cases, they take us for children and make us swallow unbelievable tales (some fairy tales are more credible) which should arouse our suspicion and make us doubt the mental health of those who give them to us.

The True History is smooth, logical, predictable and raises no doubt, but it ends badly, very badly. By the way, this is the reason why it had to be rewritten, according to a carefully and cleverly prepared scenario.

If we go back to the Exodus, Moses is logically caught up by Pharaoh's chariots and taken back to Egypt, where the Hebrews are still slaves. The Santorini, which is called Thera, erupts when it wants and the Promised Land is a sweet dream. This is a non-event.

On August 2nd, 216 BC (in our history), Hannibal crushed the Roman legions in Cannae, without the help of his elephants, in a battle which is still studied in military schools. Nearly 53,000 legionaries and 5,500 riders die in fight, and 6,000 in the Carthaginian army. The victory is complete and the road to Rome is open. Maharbal, chief of the Numidian cavalry, asks Hannibal if he is allowed to chase Consul Varro, who has escaped with 70 surviving riders. Hannibal replies simply: "Roma delenda est" (Rome must be destroyed). He also recommends attacking the Servian wall, without waiting for him, by the agger of the Northern perimeter that the Romans cannot defend because they do not have enough reserves. On his way, he leaves the wounded and the prisoners in Capua, which is already acquired, and marches on Rome which Maharbal has already invested and burns it completely. Once Rome destroyed and reduced to ashes, he goes back to Capua. Carthage does not have any Mediterranean rival left and Baal is the conquerors' god.

Baal and its local names, Baal Bek and Baal Zebub (Beelzebub) overcome Zeus, Jupiter, Osiris and Yahweh. Monotheism will remain confidential.

In 1428, the English hold the Northern half of the kingdom of France. In October, they lay siege in front of Orleans, a fortified city which controls one of the two bridges on the river Loire (the other is in Nantes). In spring 1429, the French lack supplies: their situation is desperate. In May, the city is caught by the English. They cross the river Loire and attack Chinon, where Dauphin

The battle of Cannae.

Charles is prisoner. Then they make the junction with Aquitaine, already under English control. The English archers, who have done so much harm to the French knights in Crécy and Azincourt can one last time give their opponents the finger, which was cut off when they were taken prisoners, to prevent them from shooting their arrows. The Hundred Years War between the Plantagenets and the Capetians is over; it has only lasted 92 years. In November 1429, Henri VI is crowned king of England in Westminster. In December 1431, he is crowned King of France in Rheims. He becomes the first sovereign of the Double-Kingdom; his arms are the leopard and the lily. From 1337 on, his ancestor Edouard III, son of Edouard II and Isabelle of France, had claimed the kingdom of France and quartered his arms (leopards: 3 for England, 2 for Normandy and 1 for Aquitaine) in order to insert the arms of

Arms of Henry V, King of France and England.

France (the lily). The Scots, once allied to the French, and the Armagnacs are submitted, Champagne is attached, the Burgundians become vassals. The Double Crown will dominate the world for more than five hundred years.

The new king, son of a sister (Catherine de Valois) of Dauphin Charles and descendant of Philippe le Bel (by Isabelle de France, well-named) prefers to settle in Paris rather than on the banks of the river Thames, to benefit from a larger capital city and a milder climate. The Franco-Norman language, imported by the Normans into England, is still the official language of the two kingdoms, as shown by the motto of the Order of the Garter (*Honi soit qui mal y pense*). The Anglo-Saxon, popular language made of Batavian and Danish words, is reduced to a regional dialect like the *langue d'Oc* in the South of France, and also despised.

Christophe Morley writes a blank verse historic play to the glory of Henri VI. However, in the New History, Christopher Marlowe will be killed (precisely speared) in 1593 and Shake-Speare, in English this time, will write Henry VI again as a tragedy with the new historical events, including the character of Joan of Arc. On his coat of arms, we can see a falcon shaking the wings and holding a spear, and the old French motto: Non sainz droict. That means that he – or his accomplice – was right to shake to death a spear in Marlowe's right eye (he died so), because Marlowe – spy of Queen Elizabeth I and true 007 at that time – would never have allowed Shakespeare to plagiarize his own plays as long as he was alive.

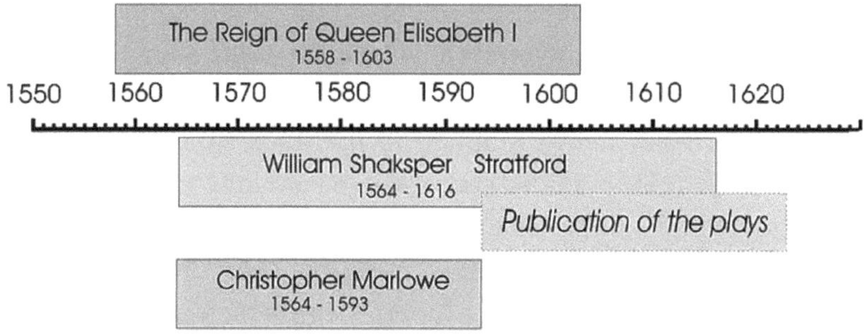

Publication of the Shakespeare's plays after Marlowe's death.

Wars or simple rivalries with the Dutch and the Spaniards will be frequent and these European kingdoms with powerful fleets will share out the world overseas. The Franco-English will take the lion's share by colonizing most of Africa, the West Indies and the whole North America. Cars and trains will run on the left like the knights who galloped on the left during the tournaments and held their spears with their right arm, for most of them were right-handed like the men of today. Rugby will be played from England down to Aquitaine, where it persists in the New History. The stick game (cricket) will cross the Atlantic Ocean and will conquer North America, where it is still played in the New History (base-ball). The Basque beret will equip the Franco-English army during the Second World War and will be worn by the Franco-English team at the Olympic Games in 1948.

But two deadly dangers were going to threaten one day the Double-Kingdom, which nothing seemed able to shake. On one side, German nationalism, whose jealousy of its flourishing colonies will soon be made worse by the rise of Nazism, and on the other side Russian communism which, in the guise of internationalism, was going to start conquering the world. Weakened by its victory in the First World War won with the support of its American colony, the Double-Kingdom collapsed on the continent in May 1940 and survived thanks to the boarding of a part of its army towards England, and to the escape of the Mediterranean fleet towards Mers-el-Kebir and Gibraltar. As it was courageously resisting the Blitz, it was stabbed in the back by the American colony which, taking advantage of the weakening of the tutelary power, declared its independence on July 4, 1940, then its neutrality in the conflict. The brand new American Republic could not however avoid the war against Japan, from which an air and sea battle group attacked by surprise Pearl Harbor.

The salvation seemed to come from the Russian campaign which saw the Germans, at first triumphant, then retreat in front of the Red Army and the terrible Russian winter. As Napoleon Bonaparte never left Corsica because there was no French revolution, Hitler was not instructed by the precedent of the French retreat from Russia, and, even if he had known, he would have persevered in his madness. The war could have stopped on July 20, 1944, when Hitler was pulverized by the bomb laid by Stauffenberg at the headquarters of Rastenburg in Eastern Prussia. But the peace proposed by the new chancellor is rejected by Stalin who takes advantage of the Wehrmacht's confusion to rush on Berlin, while the Franco-English landings from Africa (Marshal Alphonse Juin) and from England itself (Marshal Bernard Montgomery, an Englishman of Norman origin) are trying to gather in Paris. The landing on the beaches of Pas-de-Calais (the closest from England) in June 1944 encountered strong resistance, all the more as Hitler had logically sent reinforcements of tanks (Tiger tanks), and as Rommel stays on the place after the successful attack against the Führer (instead of being "suicided" by him). So the invasion progresses slowly and with heavy losses. The German rout on the Eastern front and their fierce resistance on the Western front will allow the Russians to reach Paris, which will finally be liberated at the same time by the two armies.

Then the Soviets cynically refuse to leave the part of France they occupy: Paris remains cut into two parts. Then, seeing the more and more numerous escapes of the Parisians to the Western zone, the Russians build a wall which crosses the capital entirely: the wall of shame. The Americans then understand their mistake of being neutral in the conflict and massively support the Double-Kingdom which has lost Eastern France. But it is too late and the seeds of the Third World War are sown. The new Queen of France and England cannot be crowned in Reims and the Court is divided between the Louvre, empty during the war and now too risky, and Buckingham. The Russian communists install rockets on the French ground, and, with the help of the French Communist Party, create the French Democratic Republic with East-Paris as capital, which is close, at the bank of the Rhine River, to the German Democratic Republic of which Berlin, or what remains of it, is the capital city. Afterwards they attack the colonies of the Double-Kingdom by creating armies of national liberation or by fomenting communist guerillas as far as Central America. Soon they install rockets in Cuba and threaten directly the Republic of North America. Only the balance of terror will slow for some time the invasion of the North-American territory.

The Americans have blown belatedly their first atomic bomb in 1949, and they are exhausted after a long war against Japan, very expensive in men and equipment. Each island of the archipelago has had to be won at the cost of bloody landings, and the bombing of Tokyo, as violent and devastating as the Dresden bombing in Germany, has not shaken the Japanese resolution. In 1947 the Emperor of Japan agrees to capitulate, after having lost most of his land army. Therefore it is a battle-hardened, but bloodless America which must face the new threat on its borders. The Cuba blockade and President Kennedy's nuclear bluff will not be credible, and the Russians remain in Cuba. Fourth president of North America (the first was Roosevelt in 1940), Kennedy is even assassinated in 1963 by Lee Harvey Oswald, an American KGB's agent, who had emigrated into Soviet Union where he had married a Russian woman (Marina), and from where he comes back during the crisis of Cuba, in charge of this mission. The Cold War shifts then from peaceful coexistence to hostile coexistence.

The old European colonies have access one after the other to independence and let some totalitarian regimes subservient to Moscow settle, in euphoria or terror. The rivalry of both systems even moves on the Moon, where the Russians land shortly after the Americans. The Wall of Paris will not fall, in spite of the economic, cultural and political war which is waged by the Americans, the Franco-English and some other nations, only free and truly democratic countries (the Double-Kingdom is a constitutional monarchy with an elected parliament) against the Communist world led with an iron hand by Moscow.

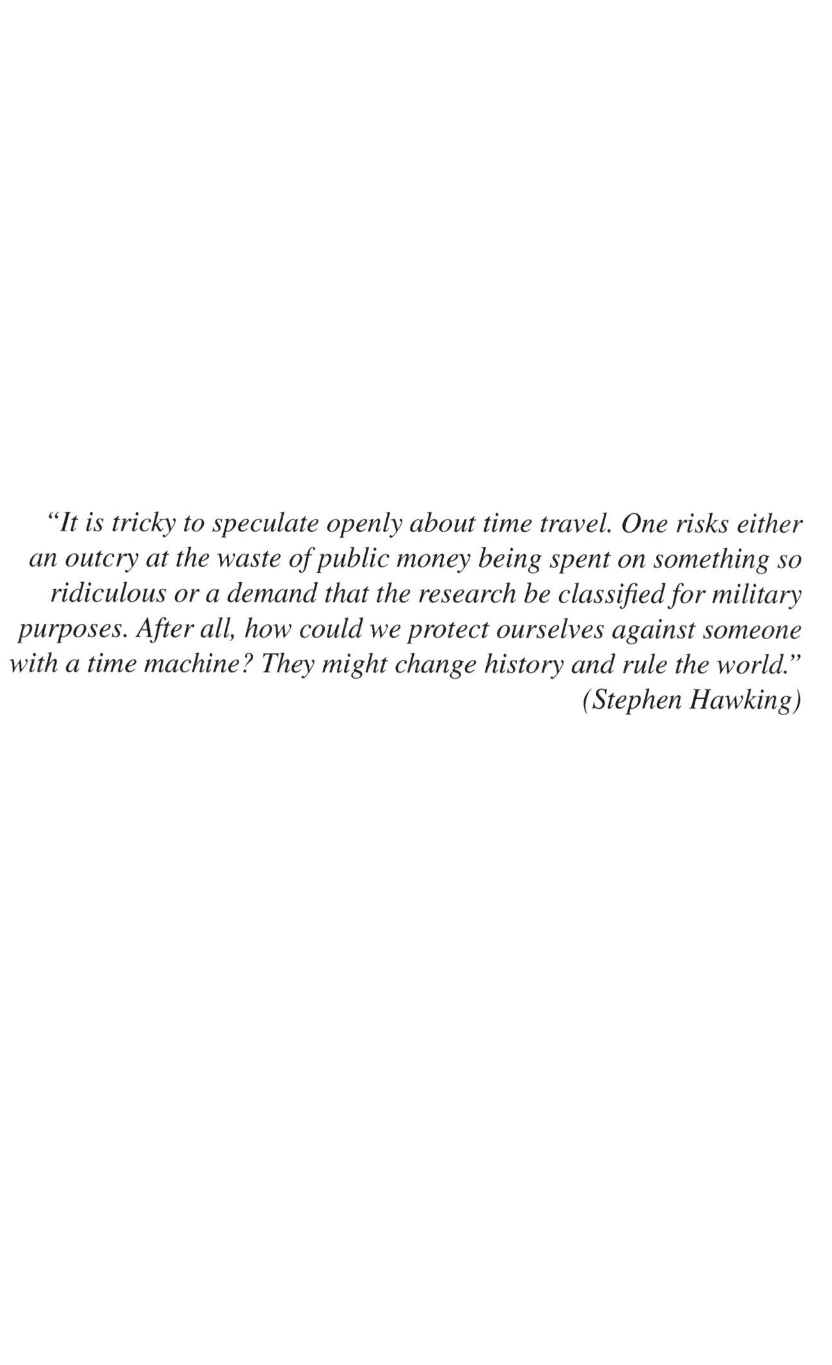

"It is tricky to speculate openly about time travel. One risks either an outcry at the waste of public money being spent on something so ridiculous or a demand that the research be classified for military purposes. After all, how could we protect ourselves against someone with a time machine? They might change history and rule the world."
(Stephen Hawking)

THE MACHINE:
END OF THE TRUE HISTORY

The situation is extremely tense and the armies are ready for war, when the Russian Intelligence services learn at the beginning of the twenty-first century that the Americans have discovered a process to control nuclear fusion much higher than the tokomaks developed in the USSR, giving them access to a source of unlimited energy. The Z-machine was built in 2005 by a military laboratory near Los Alamos, in New Mexico, where the first atomic bomb was made, with the initial aim to test the resistance of the warheads to X-rays, which, in the scenario called Star Wars, would be supposed to annihilate the destroying ability of the enemy's missiles. To produce an intense flash of X-rays, the capitalist scientists used a cage of tungsten wires thinner than hair, submitted to an electrical impulse of staggering intensity: more than 20 million amps! The surprise, but all great discoveries are accidental, was to obtain a plasma over 2 billion degrees.

The Franco-English authors had invented a word for this kind of discovery, serendipity, from a Persian tale which tells the story of the Three Princes of Serendip (Ceylon), where the three princes keep finding what they are not looking for.

At such a temperature, one can merge stable, non-radioactive atoms (such as boron and hydrogen), without emission of neutrons (aneutronic fusion) and recover directly the energy of plasma thanks to an inducting electric generator. As the plasma obtained reissues 3 to 4 times more energy than what it receives, the electricity produced is much higher than the one discharged by the capacitors and the spark plugs necessary for the starting electric pulse. One just had to reproduce regularly hyper intense electrical pulse (every 10 seconds approximately) to maintain the process of fusion, and replace the capacitors immersed in an enormous pool (for insulation) by less cumbersome magnetic coils with a 50 times greater loading capacity, like the ones developed in 2001 by the Franco-English military laboratory of Gramat, in Aquitaine. Some coins store the current to discharge on the target and the plasma induces a current in the receiving coil: we are back to square one.

The production of almost inexhaustible and without radioactive waste electrical energy by the Z-machine would have, in addition to a very positive impact on the environment, three technological consequences which would upset the balance of terror and rush the entrance in World War III, as soon as the Russians would distinguish this imbalance and could not compensate by their usual spying skills. The first consequence was the making of the Z-bomb, a kind of clean H-bomb, which does not contaminate the battlefield and allows vitrifying the opponent, without changing the earth into radioactive garbage for ever and ever. The nuclear war was getting possible, because less suicidal.

The second consequence was to make finally the MHD aerodyne, which functions through a magneto hydrodynamic accelerator with external flow of ionized air, imagined by the physicist Jean-Pierre Petit on the basis of the observation of flying saucers. According to him, the two rows of luminous "portholes" described by the witnesses were actually rows of anodes and cathodes, aimed at ionizing the air under the form of superfluid plasma sliding on the walls of the saucer, which is then literally sucked upwards without resistance of atmospheric gases. To realize it, it was necessary to bring a very powerful source of energy on board, and the Z-machine brought the solution. Although the first MHD-gas aerodyne was as big as a football field and caricatured the UFOs from which it was inspired, its aerodynamic qualities were so amazing that it could only be used at first as an unmanned combat drone. The superiority of the American Air Force was going to become overwhelming, not mentioning the underwater application which could be done. This second consequence was going to precipitate the onset of war. The Politburo, feeling that the German and Russian spies and engineers were struggling this time without success to catch up technologically with the Americans in spite of the enormous resources they were disposing of, to the detriment of the living standards of the population, decided to trigger World War III before it was too late.

Eventually the third consequence was going to save the free world and the whole world in fact, at the cost of an unprecedented huge strategic plan ambitioning more or less to rewrite history in order to erase the drama that could not be avoided any longer. The Z-machine brought the fabulous energy required to travel back in time. The time-exploring machine was imagined for the first time by the Franco-English writer H.G. Wells in a science-fiction novel published in 1895. The restricted relativity discovered by Einstein in 1905 allowed formulating the Langevin twins' paradox: One twin left the Earth aboard a rocket flying at a speed close to the speed of light. When he came back to the Earth, he found his brother much older than him, because time had slowed down (dilated) with the speed of the rocket. Therefore extreme speed was becoming a way of travelling in the future. In 2009, a Franco-English psychiatrist, Jean-Bruno Méric, postulated that evolution had been using for a long time, for the preservation of species, restricted relativity, through the open lines of force of what he called "brain magnetosphere", while its closed force lines held the panorama of episodic memory (personal story) in a kind of electromagnetic net.

Brain magnetosphere itself was produced by a natural electromagnet compound within the brain hemispheres by Papez circuits (two large closed circuits leading nerve impulses within each hemisphere), acting as a Helmholtz coil, and by a core of circulating iron (hemoglobin of arterial blood), worked out by evolution explaining the aberrant course of the carotid arteries. A little bit of critical anatomy showed actually that a high aorta protected by the cervical spine would have been more effective than two carotids exposed to fangs of predators, digging an unlikely gallery in the petrous bone, protruding at the polygon of Willis and going outwards on the floor of the skull under the name of Sylvian arteries… Except if a decisive adaptive advantage was proved to be superior to all these problems. The advantage, according to him, was that this trip had the incomparable merit to cross the lower part of the Papez circuits in one direction, then in the other, and to provide, in an original form, the iron core essential to the operation of any good electromagnet.

The electromagnetic emission of open force lines by the brain magnetosphere moving at the speed of light would play for Man the role of Langevin's twin, in that case the role of an explorer of the near future, and would alert him unconsciously (indefinable emotion, premonitory dream) about the dangers threatening him, in order to let him behave in the aim of avoiding risky behaviors. This theory attempted to explain the experiment made at Utrecht University in 1997, which showed on the curve of skin conductance a foreboding peak occurring only before the conscious emotion born of the perception of a scary picture and not of a neutral picture (though randomly distributed): This did mean that the test subject's brain had seen the picture before it was projected. Similarly, the premonitory dream of Calpurnia, Julius Caesar's wife, who dreamt during the night before the Ides of March that her husband was stabbed in her arms (according to the Latin historian Suetonius) does show that a part of her had seen the scene as it occurred the next day (true history). But if Julius Caesar had yielded to Calpurnia entreaties, even only by putting on a breastplate under his toga, he would not have died, pierced by twenty-three stabs at the Senate, and the new history would have crushed the first one, although we do know that it existed.

The real history, the American scientists thought, can then be erased if we modify the behavior of its figures by acting upstream that is to say by going back in time! They also made the bet that an occasional intervention at a precise moment of history would only change this event and its strict consequences without disrupting the rest of the world. So they bet on certain inertia of time and of the global and individual destiny, except though for the explorer himself, who violated a fundamental rule and could not live three times: once in the True History and twice in the New History he had already lived and modified. That is why Gabriel Michael did not survive his birth; he had already lived too long and could not leave one day for his mission without running the risk of meeting himself. The scientists clearly bet against the theory of chaos, which would have meant that a simple flap of a butterfly wing introduced in the past would induce a storm at the other side of history. History was not a weather forecast and the time explorer could drop a spoon in the past without inducing a disaster. The neurotic vision of time gave way to a pragmatic vision. The apparent chaos was therefore structured, directed, as if a global destiny was leading humanity towards progress, like the trunk of a tree, going up towards the sky and light, with an arborization around it left to chance and diversity (the leaves of a tree) and hiding the trunk. As well as a fantastic energy was to be spent to go back in time, they had to intervene heavily and as early as possible upon historical events in order to alter their course, and yet they only intervened on arborization and not on the trunk which remained stable and upright.

The American scientists first decided to copy nature, inspired by biomimicry, a scientific discipline theorized in 1997 by the Jewish biologist Benyus. They understood that the principle experienced by nature through millions of years of evolution, was to detach a part of oneself, the open force lines of the brain magnetosphere, and that this portion only would move at the speed of light to explore the future, taking advantage of time dilation. They had to act upon Langevin's mobile twin. Concerning the exploration of past, they thought, with very American pragmatism, that it was enough to cross the speed of light barrier, although it was known to be impassable. They pointed out that the sound barrier had actually been crossed, at the cost of a terrible "bang" and lots of kerosene (thus energy) in 1947, and that many engineers believed then that it was impassable. In order to cross the light barrier and reach superluminal speed, a fabulous and inexhaustible energy was needed. The Z-machine would bring this energy. The plasma it creates retransmits 3 to 4 times more energy than the energy it has been transmitted. A simple geometric progression of ratio 3 shows that a Z-machine feeding three Z-machines which themselves feed with energy 3 Z-machines each, which themselves … leads sooner or later to an infinite production of energy. This very principle was applied by Brahmin Sissa, inventor of the chess game, who is supposed to have ruined his king by asking, as a reward, for a grain of wheat on the first square of the chessboard, then for two on the second, four on the third, eight on the fourth, and so on, doubling each time until the sixty-fourth square. The king hastened to grant this reward that he considered very modest, but soon realized that the grain crop of the whole kingdom would not be enough.

As time was short and the theory had to comply with the rules of nature, and not the opposite, they built a gigantic machine room which was used as an infinite generator of energy. All around, they copied once more nature by building three accelerators of particles oriented in the three dimensions of space. They were inspired by the semicircular canals of the inner ear, each oriented at right angles in a plane in space, which give us information about our position at any moment. As the room and accelerators were destined to remain fixed in space, they were buried in the Rocky Mountains to avoid being damaged by the future conflict. Moreover, they could reappear without any witness at any time in the past, because North America had been highly populated only since the massive immigration of European settlers. A saucer-shaped spaceship equipped with a Z-machine and MHD propulsion could be detached to move in space at a given time. Camouflage in the form of a thick fog, the famous cloud of the Bible, was scheduled to hide it from indiscreet eyes. The experiments began with increasing energy, and one day, they crossed a threshold which triggered a huge flash and they observed the tachyon for the first time, this particle (speculative until then) which arrives before leaving. Actually, a superluminal neutrino had already been observed in 2011 (it had arrived from Geneva 20 m before light) in Gran Sasso, in Italy, opening the way to physics of high energy particles which could overcome limitations known to be inviolable.

The light barrier was crossed! Now they had to do the experiment again, measure the trigger point, calibrate the energies needed to move away from present, put a man into the machine (they named him chrononaut). And they had to make time testing in both directions to check the reliability of the system and estimate the effects on human body. All this in an atmosphere "end of Third Reich like" and under the Pentagon's pressure, who demanded quick results to start this desperate rescue mission immediately.

Meanwhile, the historians and politicians worked hard on the inevitably complex scenario which would allow America to go through in the New History and not succumb under the number and power of its Communist opponents. They rapidly agreed about one major fact: the explosion of the first atomic bomb had been too late. If it had occurred two years before, they would have prevented tens of thousands deaths in the U.S. Army in the numerous amphibious assaults on the Japanese coasts. The archipelago had to be conquered island after island (Operation Downfall) each as fiercely defended as Okinawa from March to June 1945 (18,000 deaths, 900 suicide attacks). The critical crisis of Cuba in 1962 would have taken a very different turn. Its resolution would have opened a new chapter in Cold War: Detente. This one would have led sooner or later to the defeat of communism, a political regime more suited to war economy than to peace economy. However it will be marred by the assassination of President Kennedy which does not have any sense in the New History and will be therefore much written about. This assassination is programmed much before the resolution of the crisis and will happen by inertia, because the New History cannot crush and replace the whole preceding History. It will therefore be considered as an epiphenomenon or collateral damage by the Pentagon's analysts, eager not to upset the order of succession of the future American Presidents. It provides us a valuable clue about the True History that has preceded us.

In order to detonate the first American atomic bomb in 1945, the analysts agreed on a fundamental decision: They had to move the Jews from Egypt. Einstein, an obscure scribbler at the Archaeological Museum in Cairo, had theorized there the restricted, then general theory of relativity from 1905 to 1915, opening the way for the production of the atomic bomb. They had to send him to America as early as 1940, and bring together before 1942 a whole generation of Jewish physicists to what would be called the Manhattan Project. To do this, they had to move an entire people and train its elite, probably in another place than America, during its wanderings. This will be the first mission of the time traveler sent by America in the 2040's to a 3500 year-old past: succeed the Exodus!

The Jews' characteristic is that they massively obey the ban of reproducing with non-Jews, and consider as a Jew the child born from a Jewish mother. So they transmit unawares a mitochondrial heredity, because the spermatozoon leaves its mitochondria out of the egg during fertilization. Therefore, only the mother's mitochondria are transmitted to the embryo. Moreover, the mitochondria of the Jewish lineage are the closest to the Mitochondrial Eve, who lived nearly 200,000 years ago in Ethiopia, Cush land in the Bible, on the outskirts of the Garden of Eden. These mitochondria are prehistoric! They seem very efficient and as they are the energy power plant of the cell, and particularly numerous in highly active tissues such as the nervous system, it is likely that they bring more to the Jews' brain activity alone that boys are likely to inherit intelligence from the mother, because intelligence genes are located on chromosome X (nature), and that a secure bond is intimately tied to intelligence (nurture) – the bond between a Jewish mother and her son is well known to be particularly a strong one.

Let us see this as a kind of positive discrimination, which does not detract other ethnicities and particularly other Semitic tribes. The Jewish mitochondrion is a non-genetically modified, archaic, and particularly robust organelle which has been preserved from any change thanks to the work of a religious rule. In addition to this innate quality, Gabriel knew that the work of the persecutions he would organize around the Jewish people would develop among its members a strong sense of interpretation, which much later would produce almost simultaneously the discoveries of psychoanalysis (Freud) and relativity (Einstein).

The strength of mitochondria in energetic metabolism of the cell and particularly the neuron is already expressed in the difference between Cro-Magnon and Neanderthal. When the first, going out of Africa, meets the second in the Middle East about 80,000 years ago, the more robust and muscular Neanderthal will rape some Cro-Magnon women and contaminate the nuclear genome of the Eurasian Cro-Magnon up to 4%. We can wonder whether the percentage is not higher in an international rugby scrum! But the mitochondria of Neanderthal will stay out of the female egg and, in spite of a smaller brain (an average of 80 cubic inches compared to a maximum 110 cubic inches for Neanderthal), Cro-Magnon will supplant him thanks to his intelligence and eliminate him definitely 28,000 years ago. He is the only true Sapiens and he should probably thank the strength of his inviolable mitochondria. In fact, in evolution, the most important is not really hidden, but discreet.

Gabriel's problem was still to send the precious mitochondria of the Jewish people out of Egypt. Everyone knew that Moses and 600,000 Jews got almost caught at Reeds Sea by the cavalry and chariots of Pharaoh, who has suddenly changed his mind after having succumbed to Moses's insistent requests, after the ten plagues which had swooped down on Egypt and that he attributed to his unique god: Yahweh. The ninth in particular had seen the Egyptian sky darkened by the eruption that occurred on the island of Thera in the Aegean Sea. Four times more powerful than Krakatoa's in the Sunda archipelago in 1883, the eruptive column was 200,000 feet high and was therefore visible from Egypt. When the volcano exploded, the island of Thera which was more than three hundred feet high collapsed into the waters of the Aegean Sea and gave way to a 1,200 feet deep caldera. The sea engulfed at once into it, causing an ebb of the sea on the Mediterranean coasts, particularly in the Reeds Sea, this salted lake situated between the Gulf of Suez at the north of the Red Sea and the Mediterranean Sea. Then a sixty yards high tsunami came from the Aegean Sea running 400 miles an hour and devastated the coasts deserted by the sea.

Therefore the difficulty is to let Moses pass through the dried sea just before Pharaoh's cavalry catches him up to bring his people back into slavery. He will actually have less than two hours to make his people cross: "Yahweh forced the sea to flow back (14:21)" says the Exodus. The ideal is that the chariots would come after him and be carried away by the tsunami: "The waters covered up Pharaoh's chariots and horsemen, who had come behind them into the sea (14: 28)". This will be Gabriel's first mission: detonate the island of Thera just when the Egyptian cavalry reaches the Hebrews, neither too early nor too late, because the success of this operation, mother of all uchronies, is based on a very precise timing. The Pentagon militaries will give him the means to succeed.

*"Religions are all alike-founded upon
fables and mythologies."*
(Thomas Jefferson)

GABRIEL:
THE MISSION

Gabriel was not chosen because he was the son of a former Republican Senator, but because he was the best candidate to this complex and desperate mission. Born in 1996, former Fighter Pilot (before the combat drones, UCAVs, appeared), keen on physics and history, a CIA's agent, he combined fitness, mature wisdom, wide culture and the necessary discretion for this kind of ultra-sophisticated and top-secret operation. Single and raised in a family who had the sense of duty, he was the obvious person for the fulfilling of this mission from which he was not supposed to come back. In the early 2040's, he knew that he was going to be sent back into the past and that he would be the first *chrononaut* of all times. He was trained to control the time machine of which he would be, as time was short, both the test pilot and the official pilot. He also had to get used to the spatial control of the flying saucer which he would be equipped with to travel over the planet, its camouflaging system (the cloud in the Bible), and its weapon system (the Z bomb). He especially had to be briefed for a long time by the Pentagon experts on the mission itself, its objectives, the steps to get over and the means to succeed. Generally, the spirit was that of a gigantic manipulation on a worldwide scale of different periods of history, a cynical war of Good against Evil, if necessary doing Evil.

It is in the middle of the first exchanges of nuclear-headed rockets that Gabriel sat at the controls of his enormous machine. The President talked to him for the last time, in Franco-Norman language, entrusted him with the destiny of America and wished him good luck. They knew that they would never meet again and that the President, in the New History, would forget the first one, the True one. After a very long checklist, Gabriel gradually increased the rated power of his z-machine's chessboard, injected energy in his three perpendicular accelerators (he was placed at their intersection), and began to accelerate… on the spot! As he was approaching the speed of light, he took advantage of time dilatation to see the future and was convinced that America had none. There were only ruins and desolation, and the measures of the levels of radioactivity showed that the environment was incompatible with human life for thousands of years. Gabriel preferred not to linger and continued to accelerate. As a precaution, the regulation said that he had to reach the MHD propulsion saucer before he crossed the "light barrier", as if he was getting into a lifeboat in anticipation of a possible deterioration of the system. All the same, he underwent the violent light flash just when the speed of the system exceeded the speed of light, but the general staff thought that it preserved the rest of the trip and therefore of the mission. After the flash, the real trip started and seemed long (relatively) to Gabriel, because he had to jump over 36 centuries back into the past, or rather, he had to travel anti-clockwise, which required a huge expense of energy.

Once he arrived in America at the time of the Pharaohs, Gabriel did not see any human being around the machine, which did not surprise him. After a complete check of the system, apparently not damaged, he started series of exploratory adjustments, for he did not know exactly when the island of Thera had erupted and when Moses had attempted to leave Egypt. The mission began with a phase of Air Intelligence: flying over the Aegean Sea, looking for a Plinian eruption, easy to recognize for its very high column of ashes and its volcanic plume, and flying over Egypt to check movements of population, especially towards East. After Gabriel had passed, we cannot be surprised that accounts of people having witnessed flying saucers date back to Antiquity. We can even say, contrary to the usual interpretation, that all the UFOs we see come from the future, are driven by men and not by aliens, and that the saucers are the most basic models ("collector" UFOs in a way). In the Bible itself, (Gn 6:2-4), the sons of God (*"benei Elohim"*) reproduce with "the daughters of men", which proves that they are men from the future (there is no species barrier) and not aliens, contrary to a widespread esoteric theory. Some of them are described by the witnesses of the landings as humanoids with big heads and little bodies, this is because they come from a later future and are transhumans or genetically-enhanced humans. It began to become possible as soon as researchers created in the 1990's genetically modified laboratory mice with an extra dose of maternal genes, because they had discovered that they contributed the most to the development of the thought centers in the brain.

It was the most enjoyable part of the mission: move silently at several thousands of knots per hour in a sky devoid of aircraft, without any radio communication in any frequency. A restful silence, but a little distressing after a while, because synonymous of great loneliness. The sky was empty, but the earth seemed too, as the population was sparse and the towns less numerous, compared to the time he had left. And at night, no light pollution, because the Lighthouse of Alexandria would only be built eleven centuries later. Gabriel moved from year to year towards the future, which spent less energy than going back into the past. As the 1600's BC approached, he first distinguished the plume rising over the volcano in Thera island, and, driven by the winds, plunging Egypt into the dark by hiding Ra, the Sun-God. When the sky finally became clearer, he saw a large number of people stretching slowly eastward. He saw them take the "Philistines' road", that is to say the region of Mediterranean coast where these people used to live, then "walk back" after they had reached the line of Egyptian forts which guarded the Northern part of the isthmus of Suez. This behavior looked more like a fleeing group's than an expelled group's. He flew over them every day, very high not to get noticed, but anyway their eyes were turned (Ex 13:12) during the day towards the "pillar of clouds" and at night towards the "pillar of fire" from the volcano.

Then he saw the troop camping in front of the Sea of Reeds (*yan sûph* in Hebrew) which corresponds to the modern Abu Sefêh, the salty lake closest to the Mediterranean Sea. Camping in front of the sea did not seem a priori the best choice for men who had neither boats nor rafts. However this choice provided Gabriel the opportunity of intervening. In the True History, Pharaoh caught up the Hebrews with his chariots in front of the Sea of Reeds and brought them back into slavery. As far as the volcano was

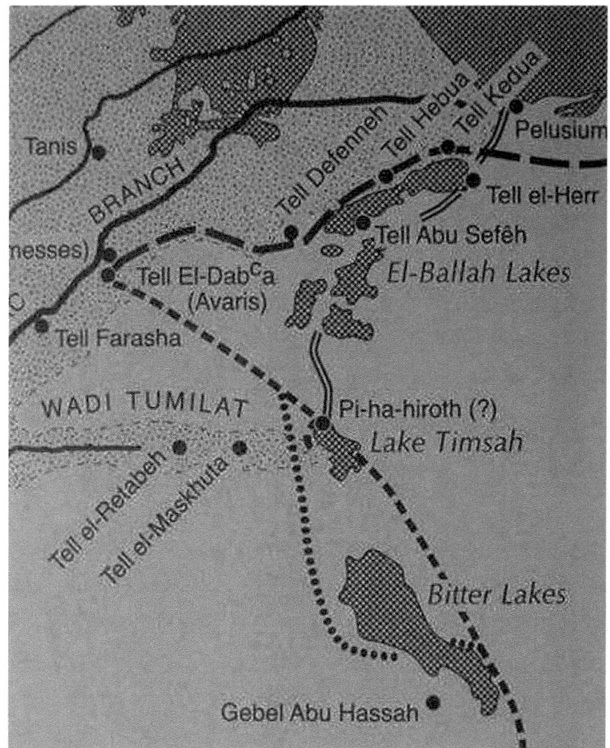

(The path of Exodus)

concerned, after having spat ashes for months, it finally exploded too early or too late. The "miracle of the sea" would consist in aligning the explosion of a volcano from a distant island in the Aegean Sea with the arrival of Pharaoh's cavalry. A Hollywood scenario directed by Gabriel and designed by the Pentagon would follow, where timing played a crucial role.

Hence the importance of Gabriel's mission of observation: He saw on his screens the cloud of dust raised by the wheels of six hundred chariots and by horse hooves. Therefore he could calculate the time of junction, which was just before dark. Both camps first observed each other without approaching. Meanwhile,

Gabriel rushed with his saucer to the island of Thera, close to the volcano, to start the "special effects" he was equipped with. The explosion of the Z bomb simulated and precipitated the explosion of the volcano, and the island (more than 3,000 ft. high) collapsed on itself down to 1,300 ft. below sea level. It abruptly sucked the sea into the middle of its new crater which was only partly emerged now. As it rushed into the depression of the caldera, the water came in contact with the magma increased to over 1,800 °F. The thermal shock and the reflux engendered a massive tsunami which devastated the Northern coast of Crete, contributing to the decline of the Minoan civilization, and streamed towards the Nile Delta through the Strait of Kasos.

Moses observed that the sea was receding: "Yahweh forced the sea to flow back all night (…); He kept it dry" (Ex 14:21). He made the Israelites penetrate "on dry ground in the middle of the sea" (14:22). "The Egyptians pursued them" (14:23), but the wheels of their chariots (…) advanced (…) with great difficulty" (14:25) on the wet sand. The crossing of the Israelites and their pursuers occurred between two and six in the morning, time necessary for the sea to flow back towards the island of Thera and back again. "At dawn, the sea returned to its place" and "Yahweh knocked over the Egyptians in the middle of the sea of Reeds" (14:27). The conclusion of the Bible is clear: "The water covered the chariots and horsemen of the whole army of Pharaoh, who had come into the sea behind them. No one was left" (14:28). The exodus from Egypt was a success but at the cost of a real slaughter. Gabriel will cause many others, including in the Israelites' camp, as he was methodically following his plan. The secret of Gabriel Santorum's intervention was not totally kept, since a long time later the island of Thera (or what was left) was called after his name (Santorin).

Pharaoh's cavalry swallowed up by water.

Then the crossing of the desert was done with great difficulty, but Gabriel had planned a modern supply in the shape of an early morning delivery of Plumpy Nut, nutrient mixture of peanut paste, milk powder and sugar. This "manna" fallen from the sky had a "grainy" look (Ex 16:14) and a melting substance like peanut butter: "when the sun was getting hot, it melted" (16:21). The milk powder gave its color and sugar its taste: "It was white and it tasted like honey cake" (16:31). The Israelites are so surprised that they call it manna, *man hou* in Hebrew, which means "what is it?". He feeds them so until they enter the land of Canaan. They are so impressed by the memory of manna that they think they will discover a land "where flow milk and honey".

The second step of Gabriel's plan is to communicate with Moses, transmit his orders and lead him to Promised Land. For this, he had to meet him in spite of the risks Moses ran because of the emission of X-rays when he approached. He had already met him a first time: "The angel of Yahweh (Gabriel) appeared to him" (Ex 3:2) on Mount Sinai, where he was grazing his step-father's cattle. It is the episode of the "burning bush" which was luminescent under the effect of X-rays but not incandescent: "The bush was burning but the fiery bush was not consumed" (3:2). Gabriel, whose voice seems to come out of the bush, asks him not to approach (for his own safety), promises him "a land flowing with milk and honey" (3:8) and assigns his mission: "I send you to Pharaoh, take my people, the Israelites, out of Egypt" (3:10). He even already takes an appointment: "When you take my people out of Egypt, you will serve God on this mountain" (3:12).

But Moses immediately asks an embarrassing question: How does he have to call him in front of the Israelites? Gabriel answers with a play on words, or rather a play on letters, of which the Cabbalist will give us an explanation later. This is a Tetragrammaton: YHVH. It must not be pronounced but spelt: Yod, Hey, Vav, Hey (which gave Yahweh). It literally translates by: "I am what I am". It is the perfect name for a secret agent who does not want to say what he is. It means that Gabriel does not want to reveal the name of his "hierarchy" and does not want to introduce himself as "archangel" Gabriel. The name of the new God derives from a verb that means "to be" and could also be translated by "is-being-will be-been-was", which indicates to us the use of the time machine. To accredit this unlikely name, he gives Moses three magic tricks, including the famous stick that changes into a snake, which impressed the Israelites, but almost cost him a lot in front of the Egyptian priests, who already knew the trick. And if the tetragrammaton is written vertically in Hebrew alphabet, it reveals a stylized man. Gabriel is a man from the future, but Moses mistakes him for God. The great manipulation has started, it will never stop.

When he meets him again on Mount Sinai, after the exodus from Egypt, Gabriel takes the same precautions. He forbids the people to climb the mountain, he orders the old people of Israel to bow at a distance. However they saw their God's vehicle, which floats in the sky, hovering, and it becomes: "Under his feet there was like a pavement of sapphire, as pure as the sky itself" (Ex 24:10). The luminescence of the Z-machine crosses the "cloud" with which Gabriel covered the mountain (fog camouflage around the machine): "The aspect of the glory of Yahweh was to the Israelites' eyes a devouring flame at the top of the mountain" (24:17). When he is called, Moses enters the cloud, climbs the mountain

The pillar of cloud coming down over the Tent of Appointment.

and stays forty days. Gabriel makes him produce a chest (ark) to shelter the tablets of the Law (the Testimony). It is too big to be only used to shelter them and looks like a resonance box. At the end of the lids (propitiatory) are fixed two cherubs with their wings spread inwards, like the horns of a gramophone. It is through this basic phone that Gabriel will communicate with Moses: "It is from over the propitiatory, between the two cherubs who are on the ark of Testimony, that I will give you my orders for the Israelites" (25:22).

We can imagine Moses, hidden behind the curtain which isolates the Holy of Holies from the rest of the Tent of Appointment, his head bent over the propitiatory, wrapped in the wings of the cherubs, listening to his master's voice…The scene is described somewhere else (Nb 7:89): "When Moses entered the Tent of Appointment to talk to Him, he heard the voice which spoke from the top of the propitiatory carried by the ark of Testimony, between the two cherubs". The system worked, was removable, portable, and will follow the Israelites in their wanderings through the desert and Canaan. It worked so well that the ark, preceded by seven horns around the walls of Jericho, amplified their (infra-) sounds to the point that "the city walls collapsed on themselves" (Jos 6:10)!

The chest of the ark and the cherubs' wings amplify Gabriel's voice, the wire of the phone or what is used for it is hidden by the pillar of cloud: "Whenever Moses entered the Tent, the pillar of cloud went down, stood at the entry of the Tent and He talked with Moses" (Ex 33:9). If the "cloud" is only used to hide, the "glory" is much more dangerous. Gabriel refuses to show his "glory" face to Moses, that is to say the X-rays emitted by the Z-machine: "you cannot see my face, for Man cannot see me and live. (...) You will see my back; but nobody can see my face" (33:20, 23). The radiologist too, when he does radiography, protected by a lead apron, can see the source of X-rays behind him, and Marie Curie died of having faced radium too long. Moses himself remained probably too long close to "the glory of Yahweh", for when he came down from the mountain, "the skin of his face was shining" (34:30) so much, that he had to wear "a veil on his face" (34:33) not to frighten the Israelites. He had become luminescent himself. He dared not enter the Tent when Gabriel got down for his visit of compliance at the end of the works: "Moses could not enter the Tent of Appointment, for the cloud remained over it, and the glory of Yahweh filled the House" (40:35). Gabriel's threatening tone did not prevent accidents, like the one that killed Nadab and Abihu, Aaron's sons devoted with their father to serve in the sanctuary: "In front of Yahweh sprang a flame which devoured them" (Lv 10:2). "Aaron was speechless" with terror. The prohibition of using wine in the Tent of Appointment (Lv 10:9) and the compulsory ablutions in the bronze pool filled with water and placed at the entry of the Tent (Ex 30:18)

A replica of the Ark of the Covenant.

are safety and decontamination rules still employed nowadays in nuclear power plants, where the workers are exposed to ionizing radiations. We will notice too that most of the cutaneous disorders described under the generic term of "leprosy" (Lv 13:2-40) are injuries caused by sun damage or X-ray exposure: skin tumor, ulceration, burning, rash, hair fall. Gabriel talked with Moses about the accident to avoid such misfortune to happen to Aaron himself: "Speak to your brother Aaron: He must not at any time enter the sanctuary behind the curtain, in front of the propitiatory that is located on the ark. He could die" (Lv 16:2).

Could it be only a coincidence that the Great Seal of the United States contains a pyramid, foremost monument of Egypt, on its less familiar reverse side? Could it be again a coincidence that the scroll below the pyramid contains the motto: "A NEW ORDER OF THE CENTURIES"? It is likely that the real meaning of the unexpected backside of the American Coat of Arms is, in a literally sense, that the New History has begun in Egypt. The Ark of the Covenant, also in a literally sense, would then symbolize the alliance between America and Israel.

HANNIBAL

Gabriel had fulfilled most of his original mission. The Hebrews and their precious mitochondria were on their way to the Land he had promised. But they ignored that they were not going to stay there more than about fifteen centuries, that the Promised Land was only a step before wandering and destruction, but that their sacrifice would one day save the free world. Gabriel's mission was to prepare a new exodus, because the Jews' fate was not to stay in Palestine where they had no influence in the concert of nations, but to scatter in the civilized world, that is to say the Roman Empire. The *Pax Romana* was necessarily to precede the *Pax Americana*. But this empire was to be created, because since the disaster of Cannae, in the True History, Rome had logically been destroyed. Therefore Gabriel had to get rid of Hannibal in order to pave the way for Titus, the instrument of a new exodus, or rather of the Diaspora (dispersion). Their first sacrifice was the destruction of the Temple in 70 AD, the slaughter of thousands of revolting Jews by the Roman legions, and even the renunciation of the Jewish queen, the beautiful Berenice, of her love for Titus;

this will inspire later to Corneille and Racine two French classical tragedies.

In the evening of August 2nd, 216 BC, among the eight legions involved in the battle of Cannae, only Scipio's (later called Africanus) and 70 surviving riders of Consul Varro's escaped the slaughter. Gabriel's problem was: How to prevent Hannibal from destroying Rome before the end of August? The solution is well-known in the New History: It is the "delights of Capua". Hannibal has to stop there in order to leave his wounded soldiers and his prisoners. Gabriel will make him overwinter by creating the first military brothel on campaign in the history. The Roman legionaries did not manage to stop him, but the courtesans did. Gabriel's Capua is unusually modern: It is the *dolce vita* before time, it is Saint-Tropez, it is luxury and debauchery. Even if Maharbal, Chief of the Numidian cavalry, proclaims "Hannibal, you can be victorious but you know nothing of the use of victory", Livy has understood the nature of the trap which is going to save Rome: "The Carthaginian soldiers who had resisted all suffering succumbed under the effect of pleasure and enjoyment."

When he looked upon the besieged city of Carthage in 146 BC as it was in the last throes of its complete destruction, Consul Scipio Aemilianus began crying over burning Carthage, which was very unusual for a Lord of the War in the Antiquity. The Greek historian Polybius reports us that Scipio feared that some day the same doom would be pronounced upon his own country. In fact, as Scipio Africanus' grandson , he was conscious that it was Rome instead of Carthage which should have been burnt 70 years before.

MARY

We know what happened after Capua. Scipio brings war to Africa and crushes Hannibal's army in Zama fifteen years later. Cartago will be destroyed. Only Cartagena in Spain and Cartagena in Colombia will survive, as the new Carthages (Carthago Nova) which will perpetuate its formidable memory. In 27 BC, the Roman Empire is founded with Octave Augustus and covers the whole urbanized world. The plan is ready to work. The administrative, linguistic (Latin) and monetary unity of the Roman Empire and of its fifty million people will be used to spread the new monotheistic religion. But beware, a religion can hide another one, the only one that counts, the religion of the people which will make the world fall over. In order to hide it and one day persecute it better, another one must be created in suffering and pain, a religion which will one day avenge the heinous crime that founded its origin: the Passion of Christ. In that aim, we have to create the Christ first. There Gabriel will excel, with a discovered face this time.

He not only discovered his face, according to Saint Luke's Gospel, provided that we make a medical translation which does not respect the circumlocutions of the sacred. Mary is not fertilized by Joseph ("I don't know any man" Lk 1:34), but by the Holy Spirit ("The Holy Spirit will come upon you, and the power of the Almighty will take you" Lk 1:35). We cannot help noticing the quasi sexual nature of the terms used by Angel Gabriel and wonder whether if it is not the powerful representative of Yahweh ("Gabriel" comes from the Hebrew *Gabar*, strength, and *El*, God) who takes Mary by coming upon her. The prudish Annunciation directly becomes Conception and explains that he does not greet her but tells her: "Rejoice" (almost enjoy intimacy) and that she "was greatly troubled" (Lk 1:28-29). The Annunciation attributed to Roger de la Pasture in 1464 (Louvre Museum in Paris) is a perfect illustration: Gabriel is an attractive angel dressed in his finest clothes, the ewer in the background symbolizes his erectile power, the flowers in a vase in the foreground symbolize Mary's

The Annunciation attributed to Roger de la Pasture.

virginity; she herself is submissive, ready to be deflowered on the bed as red as blood placed behind her.

Six months earlier, Gabriel had also attempted a first test of conception on Elizabeth, whose husband is an old man probably responsible for the couple's sterility. And as old Zechariah does not seem to believe in the angel's sweet-talk, Gabriel "silences" him (Lk 1:20). This first test explains that Mary is "filled with grace", literally "full of divine favor", that is to say she has become Gabriel's favorite. Jesus (which means "Yahweh saves") would then be John the Baptist's paternal half-brother. It is also Gabriel's favorite son, promised to a cruel fate, who will one day save Northern America and Western Europe from a no less cruel destiny. It is not a coincidence if Washington lays between the States of Maryland and Virginia. It reminds us unconsciously that America has created the mother of Christ: Washington is the capital of the land of Mary the Virgin (even fake).

In order to save the West and America in particular, we had first to expel the Jews from Judea. The Romans will take good care of it: With fasces of lictors ahead, the brutality of three Roman legions will do the rest, and will only reoccur centuries later with fascism in Italy. Titus will raze in 70 the Wailing Wall (aptly named), and the treasure of the Temple is looted: The Menorah (seven-branched candelabrum) and the trumpets of Jericho are taken to Rome, as we can see on a bas-relief of Titus's Arch. The page of Nile delta which the Menorah is supposed to represent according to Kabbalah is turned over. The Judean page will soon be turned too. Even Titus's love for beautiful Berenice, daughter of the king of Judea Herod Agrippa, his ally in the fierce civil war which opposes the Jews against themselves, will not limit the slaughter of them (thousands are killed on the spot, or will be in public performances in Caesarea). This will end with the capture of the fortress of Masada in 74. The people remaining are transported as slaves: The Diaspora is definitive. Gabriel has reached his first goal and made the Jew a wandering stateless person, unconscious master of time but never of space.

But before the rebellious Zealots slaughtered the High Priests of the Sanhedrin (Jewish religious court), who had adapted to Roman occupation with the party of the Pharisees (before they were themselves destroyed by Titus's legions), the Great Priest Caiaphas, chief of the Sanhedrin, had to commit an unforgivable crime: obtain the death of Jesus from the prefect of Judaea Pontius Pilate. This unforgettable crime will justify a long time later the genocide committed by Chancellor Hitler under the passive eyes of Pope Pius XII, and will make many Ashkenazi Jews flee towards England or the United States in order to escape from Holocaust. This is the ultimate aim of the desperate plan Gabriel is obliged to enforce by the highest authorities of the 21st century's Northern America (in the True History).

But to achieve this, he first has to make Jesus!

JESUS

Here starts Gabriel's greatest manipulation, but it will not be the last. The most incredible is that it has lasted for twenty centuries without being elucidated. Yet it was denounced by atheists and agnostics of all sides as well as by the rival religions of the Book. But the impact of these criticisms was attenuated by jealousy of an obvious success or by underlying anticlericalism. Only the elucidation of the colossal machination (in which the birth of Christianity is only one of the main wheels) could shake seriously and enduringly (even Marxism did not manage to) the irrational belief on which powerful religious institutions are built. Therefore it is dangerous to write this book which could deliver its author to the inquisitors in charge of defending the interests (more material than spiritual) of these institutions.

Pope Pius XII devoted, on a meaningful day for me, a brief apostolic to Gabriel as God's messenger, which proclaims him patron saint of transmissions; my father was at that time chief of transmissions on a French military base: these facts are certainly not fortuitous. Gabriel has seen in the future that I would guess his presence and his action, and that I would dare imagine the History that had preceded us. I know that he also manipulates me, because he wants me to transmit his own message, the report of his mission and his achievements, even if they still seem so incredible. Personally I hope, as the son of a highly decorated officer from an allied country, that Gabriel Michael Santorum will be acknowledged as the greatest American hero of all times, and will be decorated posthumously by the President of the United States. This President could even be, as we will discover at the end of this book, his own father: John Richard Santorum.

The strategists of the Pentagon drew their inspiration from episodes of History, the True as well as the New, because the invariants which link them both by sole inertia are very numerous. In that way they were inspired by Socrates' life in Greece in the 5th century BC, by an obscure episode of the conquest of Algeria by the French in the 19th century, as well as by the psychiatrist Charcot's works on hysteria. The Socratic scenario was interesting for he won great intellectual success and long-lasting posterity. Socrates taught immortality of the soul and the right reward of merits in the hereafter. He despised flesh and did not leave any descendants. He did not hesitate to die for the faith in his philosophy, did not revolt against his sentence (he died by drinking hemlock), which makes his teaching particularly convincing. He even deliberately attempted to die (by refusing to escape as he was offered). He managed to reverse the tragedy of death by substituting admiration to pity. He did not write anything himself, but he had disciples who accompanied him until the last moments and reproduced his teaching (Plato's Dialogues). He suggested a way of life rather than a theoretical speech which would have reduced his philosophy to pretentious sophistry. It could have been a popular success, but some pieces are missing: first, beauty (Socrates was ugly and bald); then, "miracles" and a" resurrection" to impress the people; then a political empire (it had existed with Emperor Augustus since 31 BC) to transmit the new religion to the known world; then an efficient rep to recruit thousands of followers among the pagans (it will be done with Saul's conversion in 33 AD); and of course a Jewish traitor and an executor (the apostle Judas and the high priest Caiphe) to point clearly at the "bad guys" in that new Hollywood-like epic.

Jesus was tall (6 feet) and handsome, as the Holy Shroud of Torino suggests (we will talk about it later). As far as miracles are concerned, the historians from the Pentagon remembered that, at the time of the conquest of Algeria and especially Kabila by the Franco-English, the chief of the political office in Algiers called in 1856 the magician Robert-Houdin. The latter discovered there a primitive audience whose rough imagination he "had to strike rightly and strongly, because I played the role of a Franco-English witchdoctor". His mission was brilliantly successful and contributed more than weapons to submit the rebels thanks to his "supernatural powers". In 1886, the Franco-English minister of colonies did the same experiment in Madagascar when he sent there the magician Cazeneuve. This man carried out extraordinary tricks which dazzled the native queen and prepared the annexation of the island by General Gallieni's task force in 1896. He himself had learnt conjuring from Don Bosco, the entertainer priest (who became the patron saint of magicians in the New History). This priest practiced conjuring in order to impress the masses with his apostolic messages. All these examples showed the specialists in psychological action that they were right to give Gabriel the help of an American magician whose mission would be to train Jesus and help him to accomplish a series of "miracles" able to impress primitive crowds. In the 19th century again, the Franco-English psychiatrist Charcot showed the reality of hypnotic suggestion on the hysterics. The motor symptoms, negative (paralysis, aphonia) or productive (convulsions), and the sense symptoms (blindness, deafness) of hysteria were already well-known. The hysterical contagion was too, by imitation or identification to the other's desire, and the case of the possessed women in Loudun (France) showed that the handsome abbot Grandier could have induced mass hysteria among the nuns of the Ursulines convent in the 17th century.

Therefore Jesus's miracles told by the Gospels are based upon two pieces of subterfuge, which are obviously unapparent; as a consequence, Jesus, who was more a moralist and a religious reformer than an illusionist, recommended silence to those who benefitted from the miracles. The first piece of subterfuge is simply literary: it is lie by omission. The writers of the Gospels only tell about achieved miracles, not the failed recoveries for example, and there were obviously some in the real organic cases. It is the same problem in Lourdes, where nobody tells you that the ratio of miraculous recoveries compared to the number of pilgrims is the same as the ratio of spontaneous recoveries in hospitals, which are as inexplicable. When Jesus walks on water, the writer forgets to specify that he probably walks on the waters of the Dead Sea; In the Dead Sea, the miracle is to get into the water because its density pushes you up. A few decades later, the Roman governor of Judea, Vespasian, tested himself the Dead Sea's legendary buoyancy with a group of Jews who could not swim because they were fettered; He tossed them from a boat into the water and the victims did not sink.

In Lazarus's resurrection, John forgets to say (from verse 13 on) that Jesus said "this disease does not lead to death" (Jn 11:4), and "our friend Lazarus is resting" (Jn 11:11): An essential comedy to which Jesus agrees when he changes the release of a buried alive into miraculous resurrection. We know that still today one person over five hundred is unintentionally buried alive. Unexceptionally, deceased patients wake up in the hospital's morgue and marks of struggle can sometimes be found in some coffins. The way of inhumation in ancient Judaea ("a cave, with a stone placed over it") avoided at least asphyxia.

The second piece of subterfuge is the audience chosen to witness the miracles, that is to say a primitive and credulous audience. It is also the sick people selected by Jesus, for all of them are poor wretches, weak minds, possessed or "lunatic" persons. There we join the great chapter of Hysteria, for Jesus works in Charcot's way before Charcot, and Judaea is as good as La Salpêtrière (a hospital in Paris). All the illnesses Jesus cured have hysterical symptoms (paralysis, aphonia, contractions, blindness, deafness, epileptoidal fits, catalepsy) or psychosomatic symptoms (called "leprosy"). Charcot also cured paralytics and people having convulsions. Every psychiatrist has, at least once in his life, cured someone in his waiting-room, that is to say publicly (because the hysteric loves to make an exhibition), for example a voiceless paralytic brought by his family, by telling him: "Stand up and walk" (in medical language: "Who's next?"). Even the recovery of the hysteric is spectacular and immediate (by authoritative psychotherapy or hypnotic suggestion). It meets the very definition of miraculous recovery, which is also supposed to be imprudently immediate, massively opening the way to hysterical pathology (we know how multiform it is) and to psychosomatic illnesses. Jesus's death itself was spectacular and will open the way to a new kind of hysteria, the stigmatized people's one. We can recognize it because the marks of nails appear in the hand (more symbolical) and not in the wrist (more functional). Hysteria in the Gospels will even be collective with the miracle of the loaves and fishes, when Jesus feeds by suggestion a hypnotized crowd lying on the grass, and explains the day after the difference between the manna fallen from the sky which physically fed their fathers in the desert, and "the living bread, coming down from the sky" (Jn 6:51), that is to say himself, who is sent by the Father to feed minds and bring eternal life.

This way the great thaumaturge will theatrically cure the paralyzed man in an epic stage direction (Mk 2:2-12): a crowd of spectators, who block the access to the door of the house where Jesus lives, the paralyzed man carried by four men on a litter which they have to push up through the roof where they have dug a hole, the self-confident order of the Son of Man ("stand up"), and the lying man who obeys immediately and goes out "in front of everybody", carrying his litter. What a sudden turn of events! At once we think it is hysteria, but also a hoax where the miraculously cured man is the accomplice of the illusionist. The modernism of the scene of collective hysteria which describes afterwards the "great swarm of people" following Jesus down to the sea (Mk 3:7-12) only appears today because it seems to be just coming out of a celebrity press magazine. He asks his followers to get a boat ready for him, to avoid being crushed by the crowd of people who set about him to touch him, although he enjoins not to let know who He is. He looks like a show-business star who takes a vacation by the Mediterranean Sea and who has to take refuge on his yacht in order to escape from his admirers. The anachronism is blatant and reminds us in what century the secret organizer of this *road-movie* lived.

Then Jesus will cure the *aïmorroousa* (bleeding woman), a neologism created for him and only used in the New Testament, this woman who "has suffered from a flood of blood for twelve years" (Mk 5:25). Mark's evangelical decency makes us think that it is a uterine hemorrhage (hysteria comes from the Greek *hystera*, meaning uterus). Then he tells about the resurrection of Jaire's daughter, where we learn about the drying up of a twelve years old menorrhagia and then about the first menses of a pubescent twelve-year old girl. He says himself: "The child is not dead, but she is sleeping". It is a cataleptic fit, known in hysteria, where the sick person seems to be sleeping, but without the clinical signs of sleep and in a stiffened position which can simulate death. He wakes her up by a verbal suggestion pronounced in Aramaic in an authoritative way: "Thalita koum!" He often uses that kind of short and directive expressions, like the one he uses to open the deaf man's ears: "Ephphata" (Mk 7:34). He also uses another technique of hypnotic induction, the tricks, by imposing hands, as when he cures the blind man (Mk 8:23), or the woman who has been bent for eighteen years (Lk 13:11-13). It was probably hysterical blindness or scotoma, and a camptocormia, that is to say a hysterical contraction of lumbar para-vertebral muscles which blocks the sick person in a bent position (false Pott's disease).

To sum up, he only cures the hysterical manifestations (but aren't they the most spectacular?) by hypnotic suggestion. Actually the Holy Shroud of Torino shows grave and impressive eyes, which, if they stare at us, can provoke fascination and bring about hypnotic induction. The most beautiful example of this type of recovery will be the "diabolical epileptic" (Mk 9:18-26). Mark typically describes the great Charcot-like fit of hysteria, epileptoid and not epileptic, that is to say without biting of the tongue or loss of urine, but with its tonic phase ("became stiff"), its clonic phase ("shook violently"), its shouting ("after having shouted"), and its loss of conscience ("became dead-like"). Of course, Jesus expels the devil, which means he resolves the crisis and prevents (temporarily) its recurrence, with his usual authority: "I order you, get out of him and never come back".

Gabriel will only come forward once beside his "son" before Passion, followed by the specialist in hypnosis and illusion who had been assigned to him. The three present apostles mistake them for Moses and Eli. Like on Mount Sinai, the "cloud" falls upon Mount Tabor, showing the presence of the machine through the camouflaging fog which surrounds it. The apostles write about the Transfiguration of Jesus: "His face gleamed like the sun and his clothes became as white as snow" Mt 17:2). Jesus comes out of the cloud with a radiant face, that is to say he is staring wide-eyed with surprise and admiration, which illuminates his face by showing the white and shining sclerotic of his eyes. Obviously he has had the privilege to get aboard Gabriel's vehicle, where the latter taught him his mission and promised him resurrection, and even not to die on the cross. He gets out and talks with the two men, and the black light of the ultraviolet bulbs ("a luminous cloud took them under its shadow") highlights the white of the synthetic clothes they had carefully dressed him in. This light makes them luminescent like in our night-clubs of today, which is very impressing, especially when you see it for the first time. We do not need to mention the loudspeaker, which resounds like at the time of the episode of the "burning bush", and where Gabriel, as father, does not lie: "This one is my beloved Son" (Mt 17:5).

In order to weave the thread of his scenario, Gabriel needed a traitor whose name would unquestionably remind Jewishness, and a chief of the Sanhedrin (religious court of the Jews) particularly cruel. They were Judas and Caiaphas. As the Romans had withdrawn the power of life and death from the Sanhedrin, he had to use the praetorium (Roman procurator's court). The inconvenient was to implicate the occupying force in Jesus's murder, although the aim was to make the Jews responsible. The advantage, in terms of communication, was in the by-product souvenir which would help people to remember. The cross was more saleable than the stones used for lapidating if he had been condemned by the Jews. Jesus shows Judas as the traitor who will deliver him (Jn 13:26), but Judas's gospel, Apocrypha found in 2006, shows that actually He asks him to deliver Him: "You will surpass all the others, because you will sacrifice the man who is my clothes". This is more in accordance with the behavior of Jesus, who disdains in the praetorium the Roman procurator's mercy, although Pilate reminds him that he has the power to release him (Jn 19:10). Jesus wants to be crucified. In order to make the scenario of treachery more credible, Judas will be "suicided" after Jesus's sentence (Mt 27:5).

Gabriel watches his son's death agony; he eclipses the sun for three hours with his saucer and consequently adds a cosmic prodigy with gruesome staging. Jesus finally realizes that he is really going to die and shouts in Aramaic (Mk 15:34): "Elôï, lema sabatchtani" (My God, why do you abandon me?). As they noticed that he is dead, the soldiers do not break his legs to accelerate death before night (in this eve of Sabbath when everything stops), but soldier Longinus pierces his side with his spear "and at once blood and water ran out" (Jn 19:34). Actually, he has just pierced a hemopericardium, that is to say an extravasation of blood between the heart and its envelope, which has deposited, and the packed red blood cells (heavier) run out first, followed by the plasma which floats and looks like water. Jesus died of a pericardial tamponade, which means an extravasation of blood that smothered the cardiac muscle.

What happened next is described in Peter's Gospel, an Apocrypha found in 1887. Jesus's body is carried into Joseph of Arimathie's grave, which is closed by a big stone and guarded by centurion Petronius and his soldiers. In the night from Saturday to Sunday (which became the Lord's Day), two illuminated men get down from the sky, roll the stone away easily (with an electrical jack?), come into the grave and get out, supporting Jesus, who must be dead, for otherwise he would walk, since his legs have not been broken. The three men go up into the sky (with an electrical winch?) then one of them gets down and waits until dawn at the grave, for Mary of Magdala to whom he announces the resurrection of Jesus. This is followed by pathetic episodes of Jesus's pseudo-apparitions: None of his friends and relatives recognize him. Thomas will even publicly object: "He came forward under other features" (Mk 16:12). Or else: "Their eyes could not recognize him" (Lk 24:16).

When he organizes these more or less failed apparitions, which lead to Ascension, Gabriel does not completely lie because he leans on the discovery of the Franco-English psychiatrist Méric, who discovered in 1999 the cerebral magnetosphere, a concept deduced from the geological anthropic principle, which was confirmed by the magnetoencephalography in the first half of the 21st century. This cerebral magnetosphere, according to him, was the only non-perishable part of the body and it came off at the moment of death to join the terrestrial magnetosphere, with the memories of a whole life which were stored in, in the form of a magnetic panorama, passing instantly from a biological base to a geophysical base. We can find this hypothesis symbolically in

Saint-Luke's Gospel (24:51): "He separated from them and was carried up into the sky". We feel that we are watching a "demo" of the eternal life promised by Jesus during his ministry. In practice, the Ascension of the so-called "resurrected" reminds us of the first ascension of Jesus in Peter's Gospel and looks, although more discreetly, like a winching-up nowadays. All the more as Gabriel's ship is not far, revealed by its camouflaging fog: "Under their eyes, he rose and a cloud concealed him from our eyes" (Ac 1:9). The famous "cloud" omnipresent in the Old as well as in the New Testament…

Eventually, what the Gospels do not say, even the Apocrypha, because they could not witness it, is what Gabriel did with the body of Jesus. Beyond his fatherly emotion, a father who had sent his son to death through awful pains, Gabriel still had a mission to accomplish in the year 33 AD. Like a medical examiner, he took pictures of his son, front and back, with a 3D technology which captured precisely the outline of the body, and registered them in the board computer. He knew that these pictures would be useful later to bring back the faith in Jesus, revive the hatred for his persecutors, especially the despicable Caiaphas whose fault would reflect upon all the Jews. A huge problem remained: How could he spread the new religion and the resentment towards the Jews into the whole Roman world? As he could not rely on Judas (hanged), Thomas (incredulous) and even on Peter, so pusillanimous that he denied Jesus three times before dawn (Mk 14:68-72), nor on any other apostle, Gabriel had to make a thirteenth one, an exceptional man this time, who would be courageous enough to export Christianity to the non-circumcised (the Pagans).

He chose him among the worst enemies of the Christ, a man who was a ferocious prosecutor in the Sanhedrin and a

Roman citizen, I mean Saul of Tarse. But in order to convert such a man, Gabriel had to strike a decisive blow. The scenario was staged on the road to Damas, where Saul was going in the aim of persecuting the Christians of this town. Gabriel did not hesitate to cross the light wall to provoke an ultra-powerful flash that he himself could not see without any protection. Blinded, Saul heard the voice of the loudspeaker which he mistook for Jesus's voice. He had never seen him nor heard it. The retinal shock led to a transient amaurosis which was to vanish after three days. The subterfuge consisted in sending him, at the end of this time of recovery, a disciple named Ananie "impose hands on him to get his eyesight back". The "miraculous" recovery converted him completely and Ananie admitted that Jesus, whom he had never

Peter's 'miraculous' escape from prison.

heard either, had explained the aim of this unexpected conversion: "This man is a first quality instrument to bring my name in front of pagan nations" (Ac 9:15). Gabriel had found the sales rep he would send out on the Mediterranean Sea down to Rome, capital of the antique world.

He chose at last Peter, not for his courage but for his symbolic name, which means 'stone' in English, to build his global Church in Rome and later the St Peter's Basilica upon Peter's gravestone. But to reach this 'holy' goal, he had first to organize Peter's 'miraculous' escape from prison: "The night before Herod was going to bring him to trial (…) Suddenly an angel of the Lord appeared and a light shone in the cell (…) the chains fell off Peter's wrists (…) the iron gate leading to the city (…) opened for them by itself (…) suddenly the angel left him" (Ac 12:6-10). This can be translated in modern language as "Gabriel crossed the light wall to appear in the cell, cut the chains and the gate lock with a laser machine and disappeared by springing in the time." Amen.

THE MIDDLE AGES

After the Diaspora, which Titus himself sets in motion from 70 to 74, Gabriel's mission is to observe the development of Christianity in the Roman world and to wait for the opportune moment to make it irreversible. This opportunity will happen in 312 at the Battle of the Milvian Bridge, on the river Tiber. Although he was outnumbered in a balance of power of at least four to one, the pagan emperor Constantine crushes and kills Maxentius who had seized power in Rome. He was helped by the apparition in the sky of a cross of light which he and his whole army could see. Then Gabriel is glad to have chosen crucifixion and not lapidating for the Passion of Jesus, for it is easy for him to draw the Holy Cross with laser in the sky. Otherwise, he would have had to wait for a shower of meteorites to symbolize lapidating. Gratefully, Constantine signs in 313 an edict of religious tolerance towards the Christians called edict of Milan, restores the unity of the Empire in 324 and founds a new capital, Constantinople, which will only include Christian religious edifices.

The second opportunity, for the barbaric world this time, occurred in 496 at the Battle of Tolbiac, between the Franks and the Alamans (from the German *alle Männer*, all the men). It is in fact the first Franco-German war, which was followed by many others, where the Germans showed their remaining barbarity until the middle of the 20th century. In the middle of the battle, when "Clovis's army is about to get completely exterminated" the king of the Franks publicly gives up Wotan and invokes his wife Clotilde's God. The fight becomes favorable, especially when a providential *francisque* (double-edged battleaxe) kills the king of Alamans. Clovis will then be baptized in Reims. He becomes the first Christian king of what was going to become France.

Once Christianity definitely established in Rome and in Paris, Gabriel will try his best to forbid any early return of the Jewish Diaspora to the Promised Land, especially after the collapse of the Roman Empire. That is why we find him in 610 as he is revealing the verses of Koran to Muhammad. The apparition is particularly luminous, probably because it crosses the wall of light, like for Saul of Tarse. In the new religion, he is known under the Arabicized name of Djibril. Carefully, he does not introduce the separation of Church and State like in the New Testament ("render unto Caesar that which is Caesar's"), which induces forever, except for Ataturk's Turkey, a slight political imbalance in favor of Christianity.

Gabriel ordered Muhammad to name his grandson Hasan – a name not used in the pre-Islamic period – hoping to weaken Islam by creating early a new group of dissident Muslims. They became the Shiat Ali (followers of Ali, who was Hasan's father) or Shi'ites. It was his only mistake. Today, Shi'ites (10% of the world's 1.6 billion Muslims) have disproportionate power with their control of Iran and threaten the West with their forthcoming nuclear bomb.

Then Jerusalem will become the third holy place of Islam, after Mecca and Medina, site of the mosque Al-Aqsa, where Mahomet is supposed to have gone up to the sky (which reminds us of Jesus's Ascension). The return to the Promised Land is almost definitely compromised, particularly as Gabriel did nothing to help the Crusaders who could have brought back the Jews with themselves to Jerusalem. On the contrary, the Arabs will be stopped in Poitiers (France) and the Turks in front of the walls of Vienna (Austria), hence the famous crescent-shaped *viennoiseries*.

Afterwards Gabriel appears to the future Saint-Giles, to whom he reveals the only sin that Charlemagne has not confessed to him (he had an illicit relationship with his own sister in Aachen) and says that Charlemagne must marry his sister. Gabriel proves here that he is a good spy, as he will prove later by revealing to Joan of Arc the prayer uttered by Dauphin Charles in the secret of his oratory, thanks to the discreet use of modern technologies (concealed mikes, DNA tests). Even if they had been discovered, they would not have meant anything for the men of that time. Giles speaks to the king who kneels, confesses his crime and accomplishes the divine prescription. Of this incest will be born Roland, who is presented as Charlemagne's nephew but who is actually his son. Later Gabriel will reveal to Charlemagne that his sword, called Durandal, contains relics (probably a transmitter or a recorder) and orders him to give it to Roland. He will do the same operation with Joan of Arc, whom he will tell to have the sword hidden behind the altar of Saint Catherine de Fierbois dug up. Undoubtedly, it also contained a beacon or a receiver. Finally, he appears one night to Charlemagne and orders him to go to Spain with an army. Gabriel's plan is, through Charlemagne like through his grandfather Charles Martel in Poitiers, to contain the Arabic expansion he had himself created when he dictated the Koran to Mahomet. Two years later, Charles leaves with one hundred thousand men and when, on his way back, the Basque mountain people exterminate Roland's rearguard, he has conquered from the Arabs of Spain the Southern side of the Pyrenees down to the river Ebro and thus constituted the March of Hispania.

By the way, we notice that Gabriel takes leaps of several centuries in time with his machine; although they are irregular, they will get progressively smaller when he comes closer to contemporary History and that the events he modifies will be more decisive. Gabriel conceives the Christ at the beginning of our era, reveals the Koran to Mahomet in 610, appears to Charlemagne in 775, but he is already quoted much earlier in the Book of Daniel (Old Testament). For his second apparition to

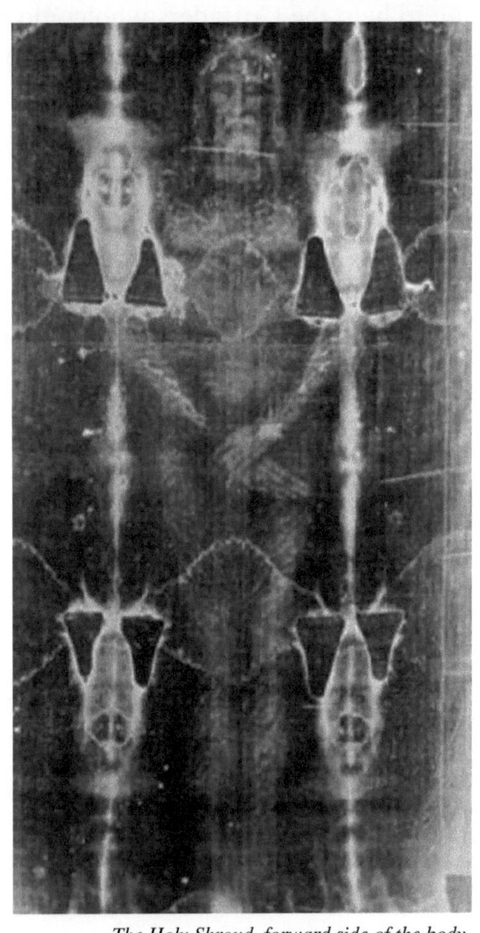

The Holy Shroud, forward side of the body.

Daniel in 423 BC ("In year 1 of Darius, from the Medan line, son of Artaxerxes" Dn 9:1), Gabriel lands straight beside the prophet: he "flew down on me (9:21). He announces him the coming of a "Messiah" (9:25), who will be "done away" (9:26). Daniel counts the years (…) which must be accomplished for the ruins of Jerusalem, that means seventy years" (9:2). Gabriel situates the event after the death of the Messiah and indicates Titus without naming him as the one who destroyed the Temple: "the city and the sanctuary destroyed by a prince who will come" (9:26). The History, which Gabriel could see in his coming-and-goings without always inducing it, will confirm.

Gabriel then moves in the Vosges mountains, in the kingdom of France. There he purchases a big piece of flax of four ells of length and one ell of width (the ell is the unit the drapers used to measure cloth at that time). Traditionally, the flax they grow in the Vosges is bleached in Epinal, spun in Gerardmer – the Linvosges factory still exists in this town – and woven in Rambervilliers. Thanks to a digital printing machine specially conceived for his mission, he will print directly on the cloth, from his ship's computer, the 3D pictures he took of the front and back sides of the tortured body of Jesus after he stole it from the Sepulcher. After that, he will entrust this true-false relic to the Chapel of Lirey, near Troyes. It was bought back by the Duke of Savoie, will pass through Chambery and end in the cathedral of Torino, in Italy, where it is worshipped as the real shroud of Jesus (Holy Shroud).

Gabriel put a time bomb in Lirey, for he carefully printed the pictures of the body in negative. He did that to make believe that Jesus's body was miraculously printed in negative on the shroud in which Joseph of Arimathie wrapped him after he took him down from the cross, thanks to a "mixing of myrrh and aloe" (Jn 19:39) brought by Nicodem. Then, he will patiently wait until the Shroud is photographed for the first time at the public presentation in 1898 and suddenly reveals the much more realistic image of Jesus in positive, discovered by the photographer on his own negative! Finally, in 1876, the negative of the Shroud was introduced in a picture analyzer VP-8 in Colorado Springs (USA) and revealed to the amazed physicians a three-dimensional image. The miracle was at its height when, in 1988, eight years before Gabriel died, the carbon dating of a piece of the Shroud revealed that the flax of the cloth had been picked up between 1260 and 1390, which made it a forgery from the Middle Ages! Gabriel's hoax was discovered, but nobody could put a name on the forger, because obviously no forger from the Middle Ages would have been able technically to realize such a forgery.

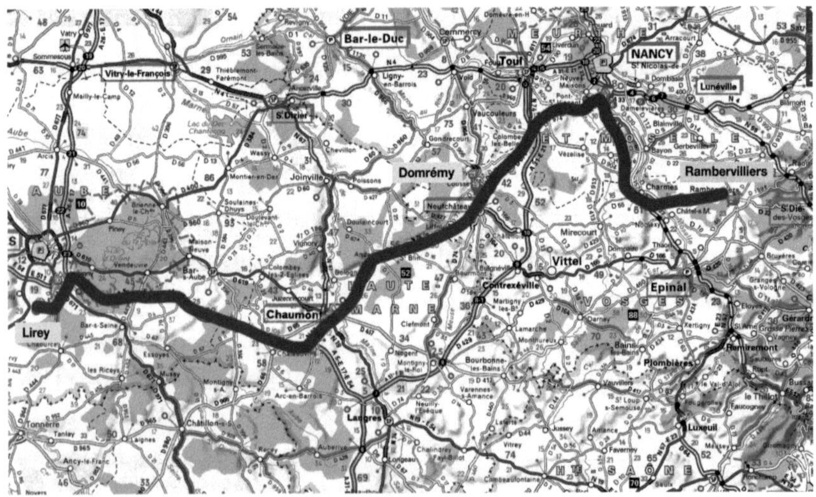

The road from Rambervilliers to Lirey passes through Domrémy.

Gabriel will come back to the Vosges in 1507 in order to help a canon from Saint-Dié, Martin Waldseemüller, to draw the map of America and especially to name it America for the first time, from the name of the Florentine sailor Amerigo Vespucci (in latin Americus Vespucius) who had explored the South-American coast in 1497. Moreover, Martin will place the word *America* on the present territory of Argentina, and the next King of France will be the famous François I. This must be linked with the election in 2013 of the first American (and Argentinian) pope, who may not have accidentally taken the name of François I! The exceptional renunciation of Benoit XVI (the last one happened in 1294) and the takeover by the Jesuits, unprecedented in the history of papacy, after the hurried election of a candidate described as the "outsider" are consequently disconcerting.

The proof of a supra-temporal intervention, which Gabriel was the only one able to bring, is that Martin, in his *Introduction à la cosmographie* which accompanied the map, writes that this new part of the world "is proved to be surrounded by the ocean on all sides". Yet, Amerigo himself had called the coast he had explored "endless Asian land". Moreover, thirteen years after the edition of the map, which separates China (Cathay) and Japan (Cipango) from America, Magellan sailed around the Southern point and reached the Pacific Ocean. Then, both Vespucci and Columbus thought they had reached the periphery of Asia and not a new continent. Eventually, obviously well-inspired, Martin distinctly represents mountain ranges corresponding to the Andes and the Rocky mountains west of his Terra Incognita. Even the Panama isthmus is represented, at the right latitude, although Balboa will only recognize it in 1513. How could a Vosgian learned man draw a whole continent and give it an unlikely name, before all the sailors themselves had realized they had discovered one?

In the True History, Gabriel's continent was not discovered until the 16th century by the Franco-English and later by the Spanish and the Russian. The Russian colonization stretched along the Northern Pacific Coast from Alaska to California, where Fort Ross (Fort Russia) was erected near the mouth of Russian River and close to today's North of San Francisco. Fort Ross and the land around were not sold to John Sutter in 1841 and gold was found in January 1848 forty miles east from the fort, in the Coloma Valley. The Russian garrison kept the gold fields safe and Sutter became a wealthy Swiss banker, instead of dying undeservingly in poverty in the New History. The gold rush was of course a very good bargain for the Russian settlement. Because of the law of temporal inertia, the California Flag features the same red and white horizontal stripes and the same red star as on the Sovietic Russian Flag, with a Grizzly bear – the bear is a widespread symbol for Russia – drawn on the white part of the flag, while there are no more Grizzly bears in this State for ages.

Flag of the short-lived Californian Republic.

Moreover Alaska was not sold in 1867 by Tsar Alexander II either and the Alaska gold rush in 1896 was a very good bargain too for the Russian. In fact Russia was not in a difficult financial position, because the Crimean War (1853-1856) had not happened on its western border (particularly because Napoleon III did not exist), and did not need to sell anything. On the other hand, why did United States do such an expansionistic purchase in the New History? Alaska was far from its Northern border and its finances were undermined by the Civil War. Furthermore, the Alaskan purchase was ridiculed in Congress and in the press as the "Seward's folly." The U.S. Secretary of State William Seward had some difficulty before the Senate, which ratified the treaty by a margin of just one vote. This 1867 vote will strategically save America in the 20th century but, if it was inspired by Gabriel as we think, we could then charge him with insider trading, because he knew – thanks to time traveling – that gold would be discovered in 1896 in Alaska, as he knew that gold had been discovered in California in 1848. For Alaska alone, the $7.2 million purchase (5 cents per hectare) will yield $1 billion of gold ore in less than a century that is to say 140 times the value of its purchase!

The Russian settlement was not halted southward by the Spanish colonization down to today's Mexican frontier, and this is why in 1920 an amazing Russian bronze bell was dug up in Southern California. The Russian possessions from Alaska to California to Cuba explain the wide surroundings which threatened the free North America just before World War III in the 2040's.

In the New History, America was discovered in 1492 by Christopher Columbus who was a *converso*, that is to say a Sephardi Jew who converted to Christianity but was still practicing Judaism secretly. There were five known Jews, including his doctor, navigator and translator in his crew on the first voyage and Colombus referenced the Jewish High Holidays in his journal during the first voyage. All the Jews escaping the Spanish Inquisition were forced to leave Spain after the Edict of Expulsion (it ordered all Jews to leave the kingdom by the last day of July, 1492) and some of them followed Colombus in his discovery of America (Colombus departed from Spain on August 3, 1492). This was the beginning of the third flight of Jews scheduled by Gabriel since the Exodus and the Diaspora, and the first of Sephardi, which I call the "Fuga" because of its Spanish starting point. It almost failed when Rabbi Isaac Abravanel offered the Catholic monarchs 300,000 ducats to rescind the expulsion order, but the Great Inquisitor Tomas de Torquemada dashed into the royal presence, threw a crucifix down before King Ferdinand and Queen Isabella and yelled: "Judas sold his master (Jesus) for 30 silver coins. Now you would sell him anew!" Torquemada preceded Hitler as a persecutor of the Jews, including auto-da-fe, and both Torquemada and Hitler were objective allies of Gabriel in expelling the Jews towards America. Meanwhile, this early Spanish colonization of America had a major consequence, which was highly expected by Gabriel. In the late 1760's, Spain had been aroused by the Russian advance from Siberia eastward along the Aleutian Peninsula toward Alaska and then toward California, which was, thanks to Colombus and his followers, a Spanish possession. This is why the *visitador-generales* in Mexico ordered missions stretching along the Californian coast, culminating in Anza's founding of San Francisco in 1776, to stand in the way of the Russian expansion and involuntarily wait for the American expansion from the east.

Gabriel's continent should have been logically called Columbia, in the honor of Columbus. In fact there are some remains in the New History with the Republic of Columbia (a state in South America), British Columbia (a Canadian province), District of Columbia (Washington DC), the university of Columbia in New York, the space shuttle Columbia, the Columbia Pictures (a movie production society), or else the short-lived World Colum-

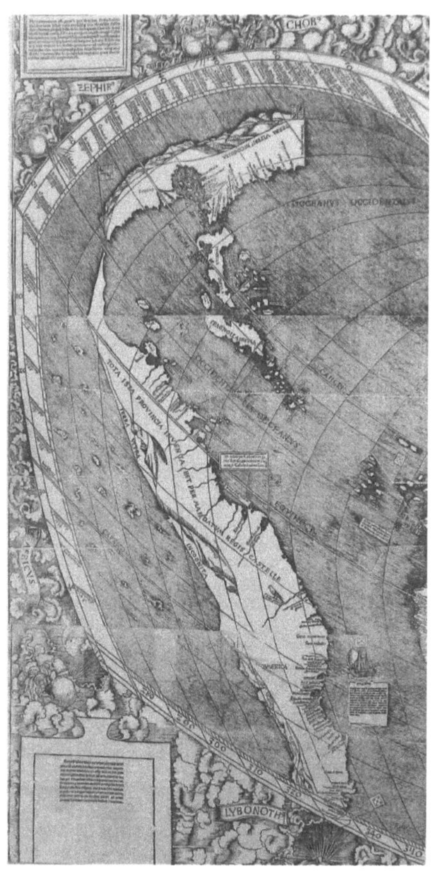

The New world on Waldseemüller's map (1507). AMERICA is written for the first time on the Southern part of the continent.

bian Exposition (the universal exposition in Chicago in 1893). The Pentagon found this denomination too pacifist, because it evokes the dove of peace. Therefore, they asked Gabriel to find a more warlike name, and to introduce it precociously in the cartography of the beginning of Renaissance. He did it discreetly in a town of five hundred souls, far from Florence (the city of Americus Vespucius) and any seaside coast. However, Gabriel also knew that this name would be one day in close resonance with a child from the Vosges, whose name was also predestined, and who would play a great role in the revelation of his mission...

Gabriel will put another time bomb on December 12, 1531, in Mexico : The *tilma* (basic coat) of a recently baptized native on which the image of the Virgin of Guadalupe is supposed to have been miraculously printed, like the Holy Shroud (same printer?). He was bringing open roses in the middle of December from the Virgin to Mgr. de Zumarraga. It is an artistic representation of a very young girl about 1.43m tall, richly dressed, of Caucasian type, and apparently pregnant. There too, Gabriel has patiently waited (1929) until a photographer thought of enlarging the Virgin's eyes with a magnifying glass and found the image of a bearded man. The two ophthalmologists consulted in 1956 noticed in the pupil the triple reflection (Samson-Purkinje effect) characteristic of a living human eye. It is probably Gabriel's image, the only one we know, which Mary watches lovingly, looking down like a Palestinian girl at the beginning of our era. It looks like a wink from Gabriel, who imported a picture of Mary's pupils on the image before printing and mischievously represented himself. As far as the rest of the image is concerned, the analysis has shown neither any brush stroke nor any preparatory drawing: this too reminds us of computer software. In order to certify the date of the miracle, Gabriel projected on the Virgin's coat the map of the sky (46 stars) seen from Mexico on December 12, 1531, at 10:26. Therefore the *tilma* has been printed just before the miraculous apparition of the Virgin, which usually occurs when the sun is at the highest, and the bunch of roses offered by the native to the bishop probably comes from the Southern hemisphere. It is said that the recognition of the miracle by Pope Paul III saved from extermination the American natives, who from then on had a soul, and encouraged intermarrying. Gabriel's aim was especially to Christianize the natives from Central America in order to put up later their superstitious faith against communism. In the True History, his homeland had suffered a lot from the installation of a communist buffer zone (Mexico, Cuba, Nicaragua) on its Southern border, peopled with pure, acculturated and aggressive Spanish.

Gabriel had already intervened in Mexico, long before he organized the departure of the Hebrews from Egypt, by importing a GMO in the high valley of Rio Balsas. It was a teosinte genetically modified by Monsanto, which was going to play a major role in feeding the West, in other words: corn. Actually, the plant cannot be found wild, unlike wheat, and the Monsanto technicians had to modify ten zones of the genome of the teosinte to make from this bushy plant a plant with a little ramified stalk, with a big full cob rich in grains. Its strategic advantage is that this new plant grows little or badly in Russia and will give a food advantage to the West camp in the New History. Although it appeared *de novo* 3,000 years before our era and has no wild equivalent, corn seems perfectly natural to us, Europeans, who have only known it since the discovery of America (Indian corn). Yet Gabriel has left us semantic leads that could have helped us make the link much sooner between the two Histories: Monsanto, Santorum, teosinte (Theo-saint). Corn is the saint plant modified by "god" (*theos* in Greek) and Monsanto is its prophet.

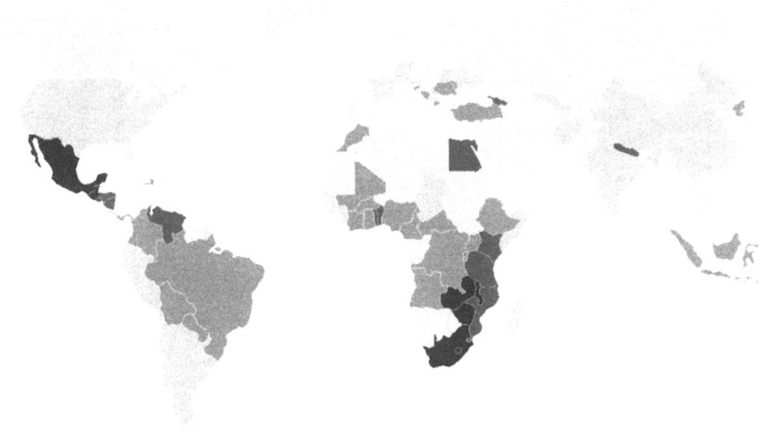

Average consumption of corn per inhabitant, from 100 kilos/year (Mexico) to less than 5 kilos (Russia).

JOAN OF ARC

Gabriel waited much less (1424) and moved very little (Domrémy is 37 miles away from Lirey as the crow flies) to meet the next instrument of his mission. The loudspeaker at the "Burning Bush" got involved again in the "Fairy Tree", visible from Joan's house and situated at the edge of the forest. This time, Gabriel goes masked, speaking under his other Christian name (more warlike) Michael, and introducing female voices (Catherine and Margaret) in order to reassure the child. The voices are hierarchical and evoke a mixed equipage around Gabriel: "When I make a request to Saint Catherine, both of them make request to Our Lord; then, from the order of Our Lord, they give me an answer". Joan will not dissociate the two Saints, Michael and Gabriel, taking care to show them both around "Jhésus" on her white standard. We will notice on this occasion that Michael appears by name in the Bible and in the Koran at the same times as Gabriel, with the same temporal ubiquity. He also appears to the prophet Daniel (Dn 10:13 and 21b, 12:l), but also in the Koran at verse 98 in

Joan of Arc and Saint Michael (by Eugène Thirion).

Chapter 2 (Al-baqara): "The one who declares he is the enemy of God, of His Angels, of His Prophets, of Gabriel and Michael, Allah will be his enemy because Allah is the enemy of the infidels".

Michael appears alone, in his warlike look, in the Book of Revelation in which he strikes down the Dragon, sentation of Satan. According to what we know, we can interpret that in the course of the Apocalypse of the Second World War, Michael struck down the Nazi dragon, represented by Hitler and Eichmann whose common first name, Adolf, looks like Teufel (devil in German). Otherwise, Saint John's vision seems to come from the battle of England. It looks like a great air battle, where the Luftwaffe pilots (remember that the dragon is a flying reptile) are expelled from the sky of England by the fighter pilots from the Royal Air Force: "Then, there was a battle in the sky: Michael and his angels fought the dragon. And the dragon fought back, with his angels, but they lost and were expelled from the skies"

(Ap 12:7-8). Here Saint Michael helps Saint George, the patron saint of England to strike the Dragon down, because George strikes the dragon on horseback with a spear while Michael has wings (so he flies) and strikes him with a fire sword, which sounds like the famous Spitfire fighter (fire spitter), which actually struck down the Nazi Messerschmitt.

After he has prepared Joan from the age of 13 and convinced her of her mission, Gabriel Michael will accomplish in 1429, thanks to his control of time, a series of wonders, which are going to change radically the course of history. First, he has to convince Baudricourt, Lord of Vaucouleurs, a town near Domrémy, to give Joan an escort in order to reach Dauphin Charles's Court in Chinon. He must not consider her a conceited lunatic, so Joan, after several unsuccessful attempts, will bring him a capital piece of information (told by her voices). She announces him, before the Dauphin's messenger, that his troops have just lost an important battle between Paris and Orleans, probably Dunois's failure at the battle of Rouvray, also called Herrings' Day (an attempt to intercept an English food convoy). Once she arrived in Chinon, she easily identifies Charles ("I knew him among many others, by the advice of my voice who revealed it to me") although he was hidden in the great room of the castle in the middle of three hundred courtiers (he may even have exchanged his clothes with his cousin Bourbon). She had done the same thing in Vaucouleurs with the Lord of Baudricourt: "My voices made me know him". Having obtained a private meeting on March 9th, she shows him a divine "sign" (revealed by her voices) which convinces him completely.

She reminds him of a prayer he had pronounced in his oratory at the time when his own mother Isabeau and Regent Bedford asserted that he was not Charles VI's son, but the adulterine illegitimate child she had had through a relationship with her brother-in-law the Duke of Orleans. As he had been aware for a long time of her mother's outrageous debauchery, the poor Charles, whom the Parisians only named "the so-called Dauphin" felt anxiety and became timorous. In his prayer to God, "he devotedly demanded that if he was the true hoir (heir) descending from the House of France, and that the kingdom did belong to him, please Him to let him keep and defend it". Then Joan confirms with surprising authority and using the familiar "thou" (unique fact) his royal destiny: "I tell thee on behalf of the Lord that thou art true heir of France and son of the King". As he had been until then hesitating and little sure of his legitimacy, the Dauphin gets out of the interview transfigured and radiant with joy, according to the witnesses of that time. Joan has just won the psychological war. Dauphin Charles's transfiguration reminds us of Jesus's on Mount Tabor and signs Gabriel's intervention.

We understand that Joan is not a schizophrenic and that the exterior voices she can hear are artificial. So artificial that they can be hushed up by the din around: "Sometimes I can hardly understand her because of the great trouble in prison and of the noise my guards make", she will say about Saint Catherine at her trial. Even if they only speak to her, other people could hear them, contrary to schizophrenic's voices. It may be the function of the rusted sword she preferred to the one offered by the Dauphin and that she made dig up behind the altar of the chapel Saint-Catherine in Fierbois. We can wonder whether a rusted sword (she will only use the flat blade) was not rather a convenient link between Joan and her voices that she could carry everywhere. We can also note that her voices slowed down from September 1429 on, when she broke her sword on a prostitute's back in Saint-Denis. Charles

VII, who believed in the magic of this sword, saw there a bad omen. Otherwise we cannot imagine the terrible Gilles de Rais, bloodthirsty monster better known under the name of Bluebeard, or La Hire, whom the English nicknamed "saint wrath of God" because he was so irascible, her comrades of arms at the siege of Orleans, obey a schizophrenic. On the contrary, she suffers from anorexia nervosa. Of it, she has the frugality, the hyperactivity, the amenorrhea (she has no period) and the absence of libido. She is a virgin (they call her "the Maid of Orleans"), she is afraid of rape, of which she feels the permanent threat in the middle of men in the camp life, she is only penetrated by her unique mission: "Chase the English out of France!".

The Maid of Orleans is not only a virgin, but she is also a prophet: she guesses the future thanks to her voices. On April 30, 1429, she predicts to Glasdale, her enemy in Orleans who will call her "the whore of the Armagnacs", that he will die "without bloodshed". He will fall in full armor into the river Loire on May 7 when the Tourelles bridge collapses and he will drown. On May 4, after the bastille of Saint-Loup is taken, she promises that within five days the siege will be raised. The captains, who do not read like her the History of France in advance, only care about taking away the bastilles from the left bank in order to master the bridge and get supplies in Sologne to prepare for a long siege. The siege will be raised on May 8. The day before Glasdale's death, she also predicts: "Tomorrow blood will get out of my body above my breast". On May 7, in front of Tourelles bastille, a crossbow arrow pierces her between shoulder and throat. In spite of pain, she announces to Dunois: "In name of God, you will soon enter, do not doubt". At Jargeau siege (June 11), at the time of the Loire campaign, she advises the duke of Alençon to change his place: "Or, she said, showing a gun machine of the enemy, this machine will kill you." A while later, a cannonball killed the Lord of Lude at the same place. On June 18, she announces the victory in Patay: "Today the gentle king will have the greatest victory he has had for a long time. And my adviser (her voices) told me they are all to us". Although the royal army, hurried by Joan of Arc, had gone without any supplies or artillery, she asserts in front of the walls of Troyes: "Gentle king of France, if you want to stay here in front of your city of Troyes, it will be under your allegiance within two days, either by force or by love; and do not have any doubt". On July 10, the king gets into Troyes. After the coronation in Reims, in July 1429, she tells Dunois: "I shall last one year, little more". And she will be burnt on May 30, 1431.

Saint Catherine and Saint Margaret announce her on April 15, 1430 in Melun that she will be taken before Midsummer Day (June 24). On May 13, 1430, the Maid of Orleans comes to support Compiègne besieged by the duke of Burgundy (allied to England against the king of France) and the situation gets complicated for Gabriel, because Montgomery and his English are in Pont-L'Evêque (14 miles from Compiègne).

Now, Gabriel knows that in 1559 a Montgomery will be the involuntary regicide (at the tournament in Saint-Antoine street) of king Henri II and will have to take refuge in England, and that another Montgomery will land in 1944 on the beaches of Normandy, leading the English army, in order to free France from the occupying Nazi forces. He knows or wants it to happen, because Nostradamus's prophecy (for once quite clear) announcing in 1555, in a famous quatrain (**I**, 35) that a young lion ("Gabriel" de Montgomery) will blind the old lion (Henri II) in one eye through the gold grate of the visor of his helmet, can seem suspicious.

The lyon young will overcome the old,
In war field by singular duel,
In gold cage will gouge his eyes,
Two classes one, then die cruel death.

Apparently, it was "posted" afterwards, as (we will see later) Gabriel will do with the popes' prophecy. It is also strange that neither Nostradamus, nor his contemporaries have linked his quatrain to the event. It is simply because it did not exist yet. We can even wonder why Gabriel de Montgomery, who until then had broken his spears *"with great dexterity and skill"* became suddenly *"clumsy"*, and *"did not throw, as usual, the stump remaining in his hand, when his spear was broken, but always carried it down; As he was running he struck the King's head, right in the visor, which the blow pushed up, & gouged his eye"* (Charles de Vieilleville's memories). An unlocked helmet visor which comes up under the blow of the spear on the armor, a stump of broken spear neither thrown nor held up, the royal tenant seems to have been too quickly armed and the assailant shows sudden incapacity (which explains his immediate escape after the action). There is nothing better than the realization of a prophecy to conceal a murder from the posterity.

Gabriel does not want to take any risk and the Maid is repelled by the Burgundians in front of Pont-L'Evêque. On May 24, she is still planning to go against Montgomery in Venette. This time, it is too much: The Burgundians repel her in Clairoix, and then take her prisoner in front of Compiègne where the captain (Guillaume de Flavy) had made the drawbridge put up and the portcullis down.

This power of divination quickly understood (and demonized) by the English, her virginity synonym of purity, her activity in fight, her determination, her simplicity, her unpretentious nature, the divine protection she seems to enjoy give her exceptional charisma and galvanize the troops entrusted by the Dauphin. In the other camp, she has a castrating effect: the English have lost the force to harden their bow and the troop scatters. Particularly, the siege in Orleans is raised, it is a miraculous reversal of situation after a series of disasters from 1340 to 1415 (L'Ecluse, Crécy, Poitiers and Azincourt), and the English army will not be able to cross the river Loire to attack Chinon. It looks as if the English football team (*balle-au-pied* in the True History) was leading four to zero against the French team ten minutes before the end of the match, that the French coach got a substitute into the match (a woman on top of that), and that France was finally victorious five to four!

Yet this episode of the New History is authentic, but so magical and wonderful that it would appear massively suspect (it sounds like a rigged match) if we did not know that Gabriel was at the control behind that fantasy movie script. However, it seems natural to the modern historians, who are often unbelieving and always incredulous, but who become very incredible when they try to turn Joan into a sheer "mascot" for the Dauphin's army! As far as Gabriel is concerned, we feel that he is in a hurry, because although he controls time he does not control his biological clock and his mission is far from being over. He urges Joan to have done: five days for the siege of Orleans, one week for the Loire campaign. It looks like a Blitzkrieg rather than the Hundred Years War: once again an anachronism, which smells like modern era!

We could think that Joan's mission ends up on July 17, 1429, at the time of Dauphin Charles's coronation in Rheims cathedral, a very "people" event where her standard and her parents have the place of honor. "He had been in trouble, it was right that he might be in honor", she will say in Rouen. The Maid's standard is a real mark, when it appears it provokes surrender or escape. It is a concept of modern advertisement, like Jesus and his famous logo (the Cross). As far as Joan's parents are concerned, the king pays for their stay at the The Striped Donkey inn. We only need famous speakers to present the event on television. The coronation in Rheims is the fourth "event" organized by Gabriel in the New History, it shocks by its modernity, after Capoue in a Saint-Tropez style in 216 BC, the yacht-boat protecting Jesus-superstar from the crowds who follow him as far as the sea and the laser show of the Milvian Bridge in 312 AD. These anachronisms, a few magical episodes of History and the temporal ubiquity of a person mentioned by name must make us suspect there is some intervention of a time traveler, which anyway is not more fantastic than the events described and has the advantage of bringing a logical, overall and coherent explanation.

Joan's mission is really over, for her voices abandon her after the coronation in Rheims (they do not give her precise information anymore), but her historical role is not finished yet for Gabriel has anticipated a cruel destiny for her, which reminds us of Jesus's. Anyway, her voices call her God's daughter and isn't she the savior of France? Her voices ask her not to try to escape her destiny, not to jump out of the Beaurevoir tower where the Burgundians have locked her up (she will do it all the same because she is afraid of being delivered to the English, and will be wounded), for "it had to be done this way". Saint Catherine will even tell her in her cell in Rouen that she should not worry about her martyr and encourages her to give up. Her voices will scold her severely after her abjuration (out of fear of fire) on

May 24, 1431: "God sends through us the great pity he has of this betrayal you have agreed to, to do abjuration and revocation in order to save your life! You have damned yourself in order to save your life!" She will be strong enough to be relapsed, and die on the stake six days later.

As with Titus for the destruction of the Temple, Gabriel will not intervene anymore and will let the English act. When she loses the support of her voices, Joan is not lucky any longer, gets no longer lucky, goes from failure to failure and is finally captured by the Burgundians in front of Compiegne in 1430. Then she is bought back by the English. From then on, the Christ-like model is on its way, with captain de Flavy (who closes the gates in front of Joan retreating) in the role of Judas, Regent Bedford in the role of Pilate and Bishop Cauchon in the role of Caiaphas. Judas-Flavy's treason is installed as early as August 17, 1429 by Charles VII himself, when he strips him from captain to lieutenant to the benefit of the favorite La Tremouille. Pilate's and Caiaphas' roles are reversed, because Bedford exerts important pressure on the ecclesiastic court in charge of the trial. He will take Joan to her place of execution, where the Roman cross is replaced by the English stake. Joan will live her passion until the end, since the executioner does not strangle her, as usage wants, after having tied her up to the post. Gabriel's trap is closing in around Bedford, who has just burnt a saint. The English will soon be expelled from France (1453), as Joan had predicted, and the myth of the perfidious Albion is set up for a long time.

Joan of Arc, by her name, reminds us the Ark of the Covenant and announces us a future alliance between France and America against England, in order to allow America to get free thanks to the French.

THE SHAM

The history of France contains many incredible stories, which are based on as many "miracles" in which unlikeliness and absurdity are equal. Instead of getting suspicious, the historians multiply their exegesis and contradictory works. It seems that, to paraphrase Clemenceau, French Prime Minister from 1917 to 1920, history is too serious to be entrusted to historians! And when a State secret is well kept, it only leaves false leads, aimed at misleading historians. The only lead that may be true must be found upstream of the secret, that is to say in the non-secret genesis of the event that is going to be secret. Gabriel can also see downstream thanks to his machine, and what he can see in 1638 is rather grim.

Anne of Austria gives birth on September 5 to a boy named Louis, after 22 years of sterile marriage with King Louis XIII. The problem is that the "parents" have not met for years and that the likely father is Cardinal Richelieu, as confirms an anonymous pamphlet published in Köln in 1696: "The love affairs of Anne of Austria, Louis XIII's wife with Mr. Card. Richelieu, the real father of Louis XIV, today King of France, where we see all along how they did to give the Crown a heir, the springs that were driven in that aim." The question had already been raised in May 1402, when the unfaithful Isabeau had only had supper with Charles VI on May 14, 21 and 28 at Saint-Pol Hotel where she was staying, while she was carrying on an adulterine relationship with her brother-in-law the Duke of Orleans. Joan of Arc had even had to reassure the dauphin about his legitimacy ("You are the true heir of France and son of the King"), although, if the count is right, Charles VI had for the best (if he had made love to Isabeau each time he met her) one-in-ten chance to be the father, and his brother nine-in ten. Gabriel had better, for the sake of his country (do not forget he is a secret agent sent in mission) maintain the myth of legitimate filiation, because Richelieu's blood can only invigorate the (false) Bourbon dynasty and extend it until the insurgents are ready to demand the independence of the American colony. Therefore, he will devote himself to make the scenario of the myth come true, with medical precision.

It is in the night of December 6, nine months to the day before the delivery, that he is going to induce a very violent thunderstorm, as they hardly ever see in December in Paris. Gabriel does not know how to induce a snowstorm, but he knows electricity. The king has just met in Saint-Antoine Street his mistress Louise de La Fayette, whom the Cardinal enjoined to retire in the convent Sainte-Marie de la Visitation in order to hide her pregnancy and give discreetly birth to a royal illegitimate child who will probably be baptized Louis, according to his parents' Christian names. She will reveal her intimacy with the king by these farewell words to the Court: "Alas, I shall never see him again!" In fact, the protocol forbids calling the king by a pronoun. The scandal is avoided for

Louis XIII, who is nicknamed "the Chaste", usually less generous with his semen, but another one is preparing.

The thunderstorm induced by Gabriel will allow to avoid it. The king has planned to sleep in Saint-Maur, on the other side of Paris. As the storm was increasing, the captain of guards convinces the king to spend the night in the Louvre, where the queen lives. As the furniture in his own apartments has been removed for 13 years, he can only share the queen's bed. Although he is now using again his sex, thanks to Louise's care, the conception of Louis XIV remains rather miraculous: Louis XIII had three times less chances than Charles VI and thirty times less than Richelieu to be the Dauphin's father. As soon as the queen's pregnancy is confirmed, he decides to devote the kingdom of France to Virgin Mary who also conceived (according to the Holy Scriptures) Jesus miraculously. Since 1638, August 15 has been a take-off holiday. The French feast is thus an ironic allegory of the assumption of power by Anne of Austria (as Virgin Mary) and Card. of Richelieu (as Holy Ghost) through the future King Louis XIV (as Jesus), where Louis XIII casts himself as Joseph. By giving the baby Dieudonné as second name ("God has given" in French), the King shows how much he knows that God gave him this child who is not his. And as Gabriel is "God's force"…

We must say that if Louis was so scared of women, it is because he is the son of the formidable Marie de Medici, castrating mother who considers him as insignificant and does not show any affection to him. He finds love with his father Henri IV, who asks the boy to call him Daddy and not Sir as usage wants. Therefore, he is particularly weakened by his father's assassination in 1610, when he is only 8 years old. His mother's Italian favorites despise him and relegate him in a corner of Louvre Palace. His mother marries him by force at fourteen to Anne of Austria, infant of Spain, and when he finally seizes power, his mother will raise against him an army which he will have to beat at the battle of Ponts-de-Cé.

The comparison with Henri II, King of France in the previous century, is attractive: He lost his mother at 5, was also married at 14 (to Catherine de Medici) and really met love (with Diane de Poitiers, 20 years older) and had his first child (Diane de France) only at 19, then his first legitimate child at 25 thanks to his doctor (Fernel) who advised him the *coitus more ferarum* ("as animals do" or "doggy-style"), to make up for the effects of his hypospadias. All the elements of neurosis are in place: a shameful abnormality, the precocious loss of maternal love, a precocious marriage little or not consummated at all, and late fecundity. There too, the therapy will come from a woman, certainly very beautiful, but who is especially old enough to be his mother and whom he will remain very faithful to.

Then, when Louis meets the young, beautiful and motherly Louise de La Fayette, he knows that he has met the woman of his life, the one who will replace the sweet, loving and thoughtful mother he has never had, the one who will reveal his virility by reassuring and admiring him sincerely. She is the only one who can listen to him for hours, repair him, sooth his anxiety, and cradle him before giving herself to him. She has instinctively found the key that opens the king's perturbed sexuality, through the unloved and traumatized child who forbade the access to it. She has adopted the interior child in order to reach the adult king's body. She has understood and cured her royal lover's neurosis, where others had only vainly aroused his animal urges. She is not only the favorite; she is the therapist who will awaken Henri IV's son's too long restrained gallantry. Besides, he will never stop visiting her twice a week at the parlor of her convent, as a patient consults his psychoanalyst.

However, the reason of State will have two disastrous consequences on this analytical love. Richelieu, who is perfectly satisfied with the king's neurosis, cannot tolerate that he may be dependent on somebody else (even more as Louise's family is hostile to him) and worse, that he may give birth to an heir, even an illegitimate one, who would point out the royal couple's sterility. The real Louis (real son of the King, as Joan of Arc would have said) will be born first. Louis Dieudonné will be born afterwards, on September 5, 1638. The editorialist Tallemant des Réaux writes that the king cast a cold look upon his son and went out. He knows, but the jubilant people believe in it, and the members of the Court pretend they do. The king knows that the birth

Bourbon nose or Richelieu nose ?

of an official Dauphin will keep the plots away from himself, especially his brother Gaston's, Duke of Orleans, who loses his status of presumptive heir, and restrict them to those who want to take Richelieu's place.

The second consequence came later. The child of love knows who his mother is, but ignores everything about his father. However, we can fear that he looked like his father a lot and, as he grew up, he learned that his mother used to be Louis XIII's favorite. We do not know how old he was when he started thinking about his royal origins, but we can guess that although he was advised to be careful, he talked to anyone willing to listen to him, and that this unfortunate gossip came to the king's or the police's ears. No doubt, it was a shock for the young Louis XIV, for the revealing of a royal illegitimate child so alike could lead him to wonder about the origin of his second Christian name and about his own resemblance with the late Cardinal. Actually, should not the famous Bourbon nose, long and convex, be called the Richelieu nose? To be convinced, we can compare the portraits in profile of the two men, made by the artists of the century. Did a brief interview finally convince the king that these mad claims had a whiff of likelihood? The fact remains that the danger was great for the dynasty for even the lineage was called into question.

The Frond Rebellion of the leaders of the kingdom, then the threat of being considered as a usurper led him to make up the image of Louis the Great, or better, the "Sun King", which was mistaken for megalomania, and to the affirmation of absolute power which made up for a filiation that he knew was quite relative. The scandal that Gabriel had hushed up a first time by the night of December 5, 1637 will be radically hushed up a second time by Louis XIV himself, since Voltaire tells us, in *Le siècle de Louis XIV* published in 1751, that a "man with an iron mask" was arrested in 1661 and will neither be released nor identified before his death. The real Louis is now 24 years old, he has not been executed thanks to his position; besides, the governor who is responsible for him gives him "infinite respect" but he wears a mask to hide his striking resemblance with Louis XIII, whose face is still in all memories (and on the coins at his effigy). He will be successively held in Pignerol fortress, at the fort of Exilles, in Sainte-Marguerite island (off Cannes) and eventually in the Bastille where he died in 1703. As far as the La Fayettes are concerned, after Louise's sacrifice, they again gave a member of the family to the American cause, since Marquis de La Fayette came three years before Rochambeau's troops on American soil and became a hero of the War of Independence.

THE ENLIGHTENMENT

We can see Gabriel's strategy standing out. By separating definitely the kingdoms of France and England, he is preparing a new fate to America. The independent France will help America to gain its independence long before the 1940's, like in the True History. Too late to beat the Soviets, great winners of the Second World War, as the Pentagon's experts had diagnosed! The independence of America had to be gained much earlier, even at the cost of a war against England and by giving up the Canadian colonies. The Hexagon (France's vaguely hexagonal shape) giving assistance to the Pentagon and the Franks (free in old French) helping Franklin: Benjamin Franklin, not Franklin Roosevelt, the first president in the True History. Signatory of the Declaration of Independence in 1776, he becomes the first ambassador of the United States at the Court of the King of France and signs the treaty of alliance with France in 1778. France sends 123 ships from the Royal Navy and 35,000 men. If Louis XV had spent as much money as Louis XVI spent for revenge, France would not have lost the New France (Quebec) in 1763. Worse, after the defeat of the English, 40,000 American loyal supporters of the British Crown will emigrate to Quebec and create the English Canada! However, the strategic stake was that time much more important for the future of our two countries. La Fayette is wounded in 1777 at the Battle of Brandywine under Washington's orders and Rochambeau beats Cornwallis in Yorktown in 1781. With Admiral de Grasse's squadron which blocks the Bay of Chesapeake and prevents any escape of the English by the sea, and Colonel d'Abboville's precise artillery, it is the first combined great operation of the history of the Allied (infantry, cavalry, artillery and navy). The very Francophile Jefferson declares after the battle that "every man has two homelands, his country and France". It is in Yorktown that America prepares its victory over Japan and the Soviet Union. Franklin can then sign the treaty of Paris in 1783: The English recognize free the American colonies, liberated with the help of the Franks' descendants (free men).

The Battle of Yorktown (by Auguste Couder).

The wind of liberty will not stop here and will blow in France too, where the monarchy's crisis is increased by the cost of the American Independence War: one billion *livres tournoi*, the equivalent today of $10.7 billion. Louis has to convene the Estates General in order to reform the taxes, which will induce the French Revolution (1789) and will lead to his own beheading. Louis XVI's death, curiously voted by a majority of one by the deputies of the Convention (361 votes on 721), and the end of monarchy are part of Gabriel's plan because they have a triple advantage for America. They definitely separate the political regimes on both sides of the Channel; they will be used as a pretext by the Americans not to repay for the enormous sums spent by France to assure their independence (they will repay later on the beaches of Normandy); and they clear the way to Napoleon's expensive wars which will oblige France to sell Louisiana (Louis's last service) to the young United States. Napoleon will also make people drive on the right (except trains which the English will be the first to use), which will isolate England a little more. Here Gabriel's hand is visible again, not only because of the triple mobile of the crime, but also because of the more and more suspect repetition of the Christ-like scenario: Louis is the third victim, after Jesus and Joan. He is also a Savior, not the Savior of the humanity or the Savior of France, but the Savior of America!

This time we have Philip Equality, previously Duke of Orleans and cousin of the defendant, in the role of the traitor who votes the King's death although his relationship allowed him to refuse voting. The rumor says that this despicable vote, which we know because the voting was nominal and aloud, and which caused the king's death (he was condemned by a majority of one vote), disgusted even Robespierre. Even the "knitters" in the stands are horrified. The jealous prince believes that he is saving his own head, but actually, he is opening his way to the scaffold (he will be executed later, like Judas and Flavy). We also have Robespierre in the role of Caiaphas who, in the name of the extremist *Montagnards*, demands in 1792 in front of the Convention (Pilate's praetorium) the execution of Louis XVI who is accused, in the first time in history, of crime against humanity. Finally, we have the scaffold and the guillotine (after the Roman cross and the English stake) which are going to heap shame for a long time on the *Montagnards*, those precursors of the *Commune* and later of communism, and on the Terror which accompanied them. Louis will also live his Passion until the end, if we believe what Mercier tells in *Le Nouveau Paris*: "Is it the same man whom I see jostled by four executioner's servants, undressed by force, whose voice is muffled by the drum, tied up to a board, still struggling, and receiving so badly the blow that his neck was not cut, but his occiput and his jaw awfully were?" In spite of his discretion, we can feel the presence of Gabriel, who turns into a secret agent (which is his real profession) and is not any more a messenger sent by a God he has created himself.

 The execution of Louis XVI.

The War of Independance will be tragically followed in 1861 by the American Civil War, which did not occur in the True History because North America was a settlement of the Double Kingdom where the Parliament abolished slavery in the Franco-Norman Empire in 1833. But Gabriel knows that the *Pax Normana* will lead much later to final destruction and, to prevent the fate, he needs an Army able to wage a long war on a wide scale and not only skirmishes or little battles against wild Indians. In other words, Gettysburg will be more militarily significant than Little Big Horn. He needs a great American Army (and Navy) both strong and professional, able to fight for an abstraction (slavery, Nazism, communism) and not only to protect the home place from the invader as the Southern Army did, aiming at preparing the next wars against Germans and Russians. That is why, added to the necessity of keeping a great united nation, the South may not win the Civil War, although the Confederates could have won it as early as the first Battle of Manassas in 1861, only 25 miles from Washington.

Known as the Bull Run rout, the pattern of this battle reminds strangely of the one of the Battle of Cannae for the Romans. Just after the Union's disaster, brigadier-general Jackson – like Maharbal – wanted to pursuit and destroy what remained of the Yankee Army and to capture Washington, which was weakly fortified, with its Capitol – like the Capitoline Hill in Rome –, its Senate – like the Roman Senate – and its famous eagle Coat of Arms – like the eagle imagery in the Roman Republic –, but general Johnston – like Hannibal – did not listen to him. Yet two hours of daylight remained and the Confederates could even have moved under the moonlight because the moon was nearly full. The Union's cause would have been irretrievably lost, and further ahead the Free World's cause too. Moreover, since Nast's famous cartoon published in "Harper's Magazine" in 1874, the Elephant has symbolized the G.O.P. falling into the trap laid at that time by the Democrats, but it more secretly symbolizes Hannibal (well-known for his use of elephants) falling into the trap laid by the Roman Democracy (the delights of Capua).

Before the end of the war, Lincoln became the closest to understanding what happened between South and North. As he was delivering his second inauguration address, he was aware of serving a purpose that laid far beyond his comprehension. "Both read, he said, the same Bible and pray to the same God, and each invokes His aid against the other. (...) The Almighty has His own purposes." We can now translate: Both pray the same god who was introduced by Gabriel. He was sent into the past by the almighty American President in the 2040's, who had indeed his own emergency purposes. In other words, Gabriel's mission gives at last a sense to the Civil War.

The famous coincidences between the assassination of Lincoln (1865) and the assassination of Kennedy (1963) are due to the law of temporal inertia, because Lincoln was the first American President to be assassinated in the New History and Kennedy was the first in the True History. So the New resumed by inertia the features of the True: Both Presidents were shot in the head from behind on a Friday in the presence of their wives. Lincoln was assassinated in Box Kennedy in the Ford Theater and his successor was Andrew Johnson. Kennedy was assassinated in a Lincoln made by Ford and his successor was Lyndon Johnson. Last but not least, both Presidents were concerned with the problems of Negroes–as they said at that time: Lincoln signed the Emancipation Proclamation in 1862 and Kennedy presented his reports to Congress on Civil Rights in 1963.

Less well-known was the assassination attempt on Secretary of State William Seward during the same night as the assassination of Lincoln. A few days earlier, Seward had been injured in a carriage crash, suffering in particular from a jaw broken in two places, for which Doctors improvised a jaw splint. That strangely reminds us of modern situations with people injured in a car crash, suffering from a whiplash and bearing a neck brace. Actually, the splint protected Seward's neck against the stabbing attack of the murderer who had penetrated by trickery into his Washington home. His face was permanently scarred by the blade of the Bowie knife, but he was alive. Fortunately, because he had not utterly finished his life's work for his country, which was to buy Alaska from the Russians a few years later (Seward's folly) and to prevent, added to California and Cuba, a future surrounding of America by the Soviets and their threatening rockets.

FATIMA

Gabriel has understood that he cannot intervene directly anymore, using voices or even a scenario. Since the Revival and especially the Enlightenment, the well-informed people have been less gullible and keener on criticism. However, he will not give up directing. He has already launched a new young actress in 1531 near Mexico. The Virgin Mary will from then on be the messenger, much less compromising, of an almighty God he has been making up in the collective unconscious since the Exodus. In front of the success (which surprises him) of Mary's appearance in the New World, Gabriel decides to organize another one, in a determinant year (1917), on the old side of the Atlantic. He chooses Fatima, a little town in Portugal, at the junction of the Christian and the Islamic influences (Fatima was Mahomet's favorite daughter). Therefore, the message must be quasi-universal. Moreover, Fatima is situated in the district of Santarèm, close to his name (Santorum).

Technically, the appearance is a 3D hologram only visible from the front, without polarizing glasses, and at optimal distance. As it is a luminous projection, the sweet Lady, who looks like Guadalupe's Lady, whose image has been kept on the *tilma*, cannot herself cast a shadow. Then she appears at midday, solar time, just when the shadow is the smallest, in order to hide her real nature from the three children. Naturally, she tells them to come back every month at the same time: "I have come to ask you to come here every month at the same time, on the 13th, six months running until October". There was no problem in Lourdes in 1858, where the appearance took place in a cave and not in open air. This one must take place outside, because it will end on October 13, 1917, with a show that everybody will see, intended for the 50,000 people that the grapevine and the press have attracted for this final performance.

There, Gabriel's saucer comes on stage for the famous "sun dance". First, it blows away the clouds and the rain with the ionized breath of air which maintains it hanging in the air ("the clouds tore away"), then stays in front of the solar disc and the surprised witnesses notice that they can look straight at it without being blinded ("like a matt silver disc"). It revolves because of the gyroscopic movement, which allows it to stabilize on its axis. Gabriel adds a nightclub effect, as he had done with the black light on Tabor Mount, using a new party lighting: a revolving color changer as spotlight, which becomes for the witnesses of that time "a wheel of fireworks, taking all the colors of the rainbow". Or else: "The sunlight changed its color; it seemed that it was crossing the stained-glasses windows of a cathedral". Then, like all the UFOs of discoid shape when they try to land, it falls clumsily like a dead leaf (oscillating movement) towards the spectators. They mistake it for the sun and think it is dancing and coming dangerously towards them: "The sun was rushing towards the earth and zigzagging in the sky". Then Gabriel stops the fall of his machine and suddenly slips away, leaving the spectators dazzled again by the real solar disc. They also notice that the muddy soil and their rain-soaked clothes have dried, under the combined effect of the heat of the sun, and (but they are not aware of it) the breath of air from Gabriel's saucer (a hair-dryer effect in a way).

He has not chosen the date of October 13 by chance, because it announces the October Revolution in Russia, which will see the seizure of power by the Bolsheviks on October 25 (Julian calendar), actually November 7 in the Gregorian calendar. There begins, after a long preparation upstream, Gabriel's direct war against the Soviet power which one day will threaten his country in the True History, the one that has already taken place and disastrously finished for America. From the appearance of July 13, the Virgin implicitly announces the Bolshevik Russia's dechristianization, since she already hopes for its future reconversion (which will sign the definitive victory of America): "If my requests are

The sun in Fatima. The film is not overexposed by the solar disc, because Gabriel's saucer (dark stain) shields.

respected, Russia will convert and we shall have peace; otherwise, it will spread its errors all around the world, inducing wars and persecutions against the Church. The good will be martyrized, the Holy Father will suffer a lot, and several nations will be annihilated. At the end, my Immaculate Heart will triumph. The Holy Father will dedicate Russia to me and it will convert".

She announces the war in progress, but she also announces the next one, for "under Pius XI's pontificate will start another war, still worse. When you will see a night illuminated by an unknown light, you will know that it is the great sign which God will give you that He will punish the world for its crimes, by the way of war". On January 25, 1938, from 6:30 to 9:30 pm, an aurora borealis of exceptional magnitude was streaking the sky from Western Europe down to Morocco (it was seen as far as 28° North latitude). A few months later, the German army came into Austria to annex it and Hitler's awful aggression began.

She also describes the last Pope's death throes: It is Fatima's third secret, revealed by the Vatican in 2000. The children can see a Bishop, dressed in white, pass on a television screen ("a mirror") near Our Lady. The Holy Father crosses a city half in ruins, he finds corpses on his way, he gets finally killed by a group of soldiers who shoot him several times. Actually, the children can see what would have happened if the communist Russia had not converted to Christianity and, especially, the invasion of Rome by the Red Army and the last pope's death, shot by a burst of Kalashnikov. This description fits in with the 112th prophecy of Saint Malachi, which describes the end of Petrus Romanus (the last pope) and the destruction of the city with seven hills (Rome). We shall talk about it again.

THE NEW STRATEGY
(MODERN ERA)

Fatima announced the Second World War and the Soviet threat. Gabriel was not going to do anything to slow down the rise of Nazism, which would frighten away more and more Ashkenazi Jews towards the United States, but he was going to do everything to slow down the Soviet growth which, as he knew, would destroy his own country in the end. His intervention was going to take place on two very different fields: one on the field of British Intelligence services, the other on the more unexpected but not less determining field of Vatican.

Gabriel's military mission is first to prevent the death of thousands of allied soldiers on June 6, 1944 but also, and it is more surprising, Hitler's death on July 20, 1944. For this, he first has to learn English, for we must remember that he only speaks Franco-Norman, official language of the Double-Kingdom and the most widespread in his History. He also has to learn Italian, for his new strategy begins with the assassination of a Pope. The assassinated popes are easy to spot, because their successors take their names, in a kind of pseudo tribute to get rid of guilt, and just add a figure. Therefore, it was with Pius XI, assassinated then replaced by Pius XII, and with John-Paul 1st, still more rapidly assassinated and replaced by John-Paul II.

Pius XI opportunely dies on February 1939. He leaves his place to a more cautious, less openly anti-Nazi Pope, who will especially refuse to see the Shoah, supposed to frighten away more and more Ashkenazi Jews towards west and if possible to America. It would have been quite different with Pius XI, if he had lived; he had already made an anti-Nazi encyclical read on March 21st, 1937 (Mit brennender Sorge) in all the churches of Germany, and made a condemnation in eight points of racism and of the worship of State published on May 3rd, 1938, the day when Hitler came officially to Rome. He was preparing a speech denouncing the racial persecutions by the Nazis and the march towards war of the fascist Italy. It was going to be delivered for the tenth anniversary of the Concordat between Italy and the Vatican in the presence of Mussolini, when Pius XI died during the night preceding his speech. It was too much for Mussolini, but also for Gabriel, who greatly needed the Nazi persecutions to frighten away the Jews towards America. This will be the fourth flight of Jews schedulded by Gabriel since the Exodus, the Diaspora and the "Fuga", and the first of Ashkenazi, which I call the "Flucht" because of its German starting point. Therefore, he did nothing to prevent Pr Petacci, doctor of the Vatican and Clara Petacci's father (the Duce's mistress) from administrating a lethal injection to such an awkward pope. Neither did he do anything to prevent the election of Cardinal Pacelli, diplomatic Camerlengo who had hastily destroyed the deceased Pope's speech, against Cardinal Maglione, thought to be steadier with Germany. He will have to work more actively for the express elimination of John-Paul 1st with the help on this occasion of ... American accomplices!

A few years later, the expanding universe model of a Catholic priest and physicist, Georges Lemaître, was rejected by an atheist colleague, Fred Hoyle, who applied the derisive terme "Big Bang" to Lemaître's theory. The beginning of the universe suddenly sounded too much like the first verse of the Bible: "At the beginning, God created the heavens and the earth." But this theory will eventually become true and Pope Pius XII declared that, when he discovered it, science had identified the "epoch when the world came forth from the hands of the Creator", without realizing that Gabriel, who perfectly knew the Big Bang theory, introduced himself well before the "fiat lux" in the first verse of the Bible.

Gabriel will first win, at the beginning of the Second World War, two strategic successes that he has been thoroughly preparing for centuries. The first was the success of the re-embarking of the English troops in Dunkirk, and the immediate carrying on of the war. In the True History, there is no capitulation of France, no free zone, no bombing of the French fleet In Mers-el-Kebir, and General De Gaulle is just a Franco-English general like the others. The Court flees to Bordeaux, and then takes refuge in London; the Double-Kingdom reorganizes slowly around England, survivor of the disaster, and the Colonial Empire. The second strategic success, more determining, is the entering in war of the United States of America whose Declaration of Independence has considerably been moved forward by Gabriel with the help of France, in this unique aim, while in the True History North America takes advantage of the Nazi invasion to gain its independence and does not intervene in the European conflict. Thus, the face of war and especially the future ending of the Cold War are changed.

In 1943, the headquarters of the British Intelligence Service intercept the radio messages from the Germans and even own a copy of Enigma, the encoding machine that equips the German army, but not Lorenz's machine, which is used to encode the hypersensitive messages, exchanged between Hitler and his generals. Gabriel knows that Thomas Fleurs (Tommy Flowers in the New History) has made the first electronic computer, binary and programmable, able to decipher the messages encoded by Lorenz's machine and called Le Colosse (Colossus in the New History) thanks to its impressive dimensions, but he also knows that in the True History it was not ready in time. Indeed, on May 31st, 1944, the first machine is ready, but a mysterious defect, probably an interfering oscillation between the heating system and some of the 1500 vacuum tubes prevent it from functioning.

Colossus.

Deeming that Hitler has been expecting a landing in Normandy since the precedent of Dieppe's raid in 1942, Montgomery considers landing in Pas-de-Calais on June 6th. There Gabriel intervenes in the New History, in the night from May 31st to June 1st, after the exhausted technicians of the team in charge of putting into service have come back home to get a few hours of sleep. When they arrive on the site at 8:30 on the following morning, they find the machine working! Around 3:00 Chandeleur (Chandler in the New History) who was left alone to work on the problem must pay attention to a radiator pipe which has sprung a leak of water that threatened directly the base of Colossus. Thanks to the diversion, Gabriel quickly replaces the few defective vacuum tubes by some modern transistors and, when the technicians arrive on the site at 8:30 on the following morning, they find the machine working! Later, the compromising discovery of the transistors replacing the tubes led Churchill to destroy the machine at the end of the fighting, instead of passing it into the public domain for a scientific research or keeping it in a War Museum. Incidentally, it implies that the MI6 and maybe other intelligence services are aware of this intervention of the future.

The synthesis of the decoding of the Colossus rapidly shows that Hitler does not believe in a landing on the Norman beaches and that no reinforcement, especially the 11th Armored Division and its formidable Tiger tanks, will be sent there for fear of an operation of diversion hiding the real future landing in Pas-de-Calais. In front of these essential pieces of information, Eisenhower decides to land in Normandy. Maybe this is why Churchill named the operation Overlord (Overlord is the Lord over the Lords) rather than Mothball as the Interservice Security Bureau proposed, not only because it was more mediatic, but also because he knew that somebody else was leading the Lords of the war – essentially himself and Roosevelt – to the victory.

Adolf Hitler's life, in the True History, ceased on July 20, 1944 in the map room of his headquarters in East Prussia, to the greatest benefit of Soviet Russia and to the detriment of the armies of the Double-Crown who, after a difficult landing on the Pas-de-Calais coast had also to face a triumphant Rommel. In order to avoid a tragic ending to the attack of July 20, Gabriel thought that the best was to organize it. He changed himself into a SOE's (English secret service) agent and provided himself to Stauffenberg with an English bomb that was meant to explode only partially. The poor conspirator did not know that his bomb was only made to wound, not to kill. The second advantage was that Rommel was implicated in the attack and was forced to commit suicide on October 14, 1944. Hitler himself rid the Allied of the only chief of army groups able to stop or slow them down in the West, while that man had survived the machine-gunning of his car by a Spitfire near the village Sainte-Foy-de-Montgomery (nobody could make that up) on July 17, 1944. He was even going to facilitate their advance by waiting persistently for the main landing in Pas-de-Calais and not concentrating his rockets V1 and V2, his reaction Me 362 and his Tiger tanks on the real allied landing in Normandy. Hitler could nevertheless go on slowing down the advance of the Soviets on the East and Gabriel had used him unwittingly, starting already the Cold War with the anticipation conferred by his life in the True History and that only Patton (as a visionary) had publicly shared at that time.

The very long-term strategic plan that Gabriel had set up at the beginning of his mission and which he had used as an unifying thread all along his manipulation of history was at last going to be realized with the Manhattan project, carried by the Jewish physicians from Europe that Gabriel had driven to emigrate to the United States. Fleeing from the holocaust, 31 Jewish scientists including 26 expelled from Europe by the Nazi persecutions (even Catholic Fermi's wife was a Jew) will be reunited in this project, which will lead to the explosion of the first A Bomb. Even the choice of Manhattan's name is not due to chance, for this New York district is peopled with 243,000 Jews. From the Marranen of New Amsterdam (before the Duke of York laid siege in front of Manhattan and exchanged it at Breda's treaty for the island of Banda in the Maluku archipelago) to the Jewish immigration of the 1880's after a first wave of anti-Semitism in central and western Europe, there are today as many Jews in New York as in Israel.

Helped by the Nazi terror that he had himself made up, Gabriel went as far as letting the Pope Pius XI be assassinated, although he had been courageous enough to denounce it on the contrary. The atomic Judeo-American bomb exploded before all the others and forced Japan to capitulate without too much American bloodshed. Therefore, it is no more a bloodless America, like in the True History (where Japan had attacked in order to exploit its lack of experience as a young independent nation), which was going to face the Soviet ogre and his numerous satellites.

The Cold War was thus beginning under the best auspices to win the Cuba crisis, which was however going to do a collateral victim (Kennedy's assassination by a KGB's agent) without anyway bringing about the "hostile coexistence" which, in the True History, would lead to the Third World War. The peaceful coexistence was going to overcome the Soviet Union for it deprived them of their main spring, the military threat, and brought them back to the economic and political field where they had nearly lost the fight for domination. In order to hasten the Soviet Union's death throes, Gabriel was going to take out his secret weapon, which he had been preparing for almost two thousand years, the Christian Religion. The one that links the believers beyond the walls, the borders, the buffer zones and any iron curtains. He induced the phase two of the religion war he had started in Fatima, even before the October Revolution whose date he obviously knew.

It was a pitiless blitzkrieg, the highlight of his works, which started from Vatican, the army-less State he had also created, and which spread like a spiritual wave all across Europe, overwhelming communist parties unable to contain it. The Red Church collapsed with its last believers. However, before that, he had to correct a mistake that finally was not really one. Gabriel could not oppose the election of John-Paul 1st, but he could have him assassinated. For this, he was granted intra-muros with an Irish-American team that did not need any motivations. After this forfeit, and only after, he would be able to have the candidate (non-Italian) of his choice, not easily yet, elected by a worried and confused conclave.

Nevertheless, everything started on September 29, 1978 in the early morning, only thirty-three days after John-Paul 1st election. The Pope's private secretary, the Irish John Magee, finds the Pope dead on his bed, in his white cassock, his face peaceful and smiling. Actually, he died in his bathroom, in his underwear, covered with vomit, his face fixed in an awful grimace, poisoned by digitalin, and the embalmers are already on their way. The only true thing is the name of this man close to the Pope and serious candidate for the title of executor. We shall find him again on March 24, 2010, when he resigns from his bishop's seat of Cloyne, in Ireland, after he has been implicated in the scandal of sexual abuse on chil-

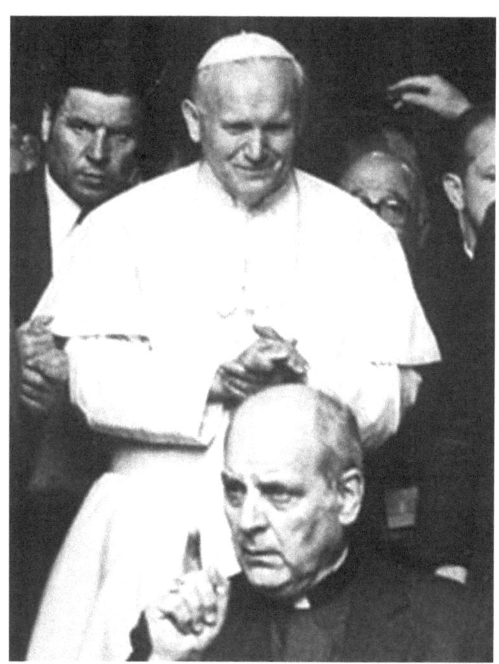

Jean-Paul II and Mgr Marcinkus.

dren from his diocese. So Magee is not really an altar boy.

The day before, John-Paul 1st had made his "majesty's trick", an act of authority as we had not seen for a long time from a Supreme Pontiff. The upright Albino Luciani had decided to revoke Mgr. Marcinkus, ordained priest in Chicago in 1947, who had become president of the Institute for Religion Works, the Vatican bank that manages the money deposited by the religious congregations and the dioceses from the whole world. He is implicated in the bankruptcy of the Banco Ambrosiano ($1,2 billion worse off), a financial institution closely linked to Vatican, whose president Roberto Calvi will be found hanged under a bridge of London on June 18, 1982. Marcinkus will be subjected to a warrant by the Italian justice and will only be freed thanks to his Vatican passport. He will go back to Chicago in 1990. The Pope also presents with an ultimatum the cardinal of Chicago, John Cody, a man with loose morals and implicated in the financial scandal too. When we know that Chicago has a so numerous population of Irish origin, that the Mayor Richard Daley comes from this immigration, and that the city includes the greatest community of Polish origin after Warsaw, this Irish-American plot aiming to install a Polish pope will not surprise us!

This Pope named Karol Wojtyla immediately takes the name of John-Paul II, as if he wanted people to forget his predecessor, and plays at once the role assigned by Gabriel. He criticizes the anticlerical Soviet system from the beginning of his pontificate. He supports in Poland the syndicate Solidarnosc and Lech Walesa, who meets him in 1981. In exchange for his support to the free syndicate, which challenges the communist power, the American Administration gives the Pope strategic information, especially satellite views of Poland. This very close relationship between Reagan and John-Paul II can be considered as a strategic alliance between the United States and Vatican. The fall of the Berlin Wall in 1989 and the end of the USSR the year after were closely linked to the anti-communist action of John-Paul II. Mikhail Gorbatchev will himself admit it: "All that happened in Eastern Europe during these past years would not have been possible without the presence of this pope". It is the realization of the Virgin's prophecy in Fatima on July 13, 1917: "At the end my Immaculate Heart will triumph. The Holy Father (John-Paul II) will consecrate to me Russia who will convert." Nevertheless, before that, they first had to kill John-Paul Ist, an upright Pope victim of the reasons of State.

Gabriel will achieve a last exploit in Vatican; He will leave us Saint Malachi's prophecy, or Prophecy of the popes, which gives through a Latin sentence an indication about each pope from Célestin II on. This esoteric text is attributed to the bishop Malachi, born in Ireland in Armagh around 1094 (an Irishman again), but it is rather an apocryphal text from the 16th century for it is published for the first time in 1595 in Venice. The last popes are perfectly described, especially the ones who interest us:

-101. (The depopulated religion) Benoit XV (1914-1922). He was pope during the Great War (1914-1918), the Spanish flu and the Russian revolution.
-105. (The fearless faith) Pie XI (1922-1939). The fearless pope who challenged Hitler and Mussolini.
-106 (the angelic pastor) Pie XII (1939-1958). The pope who showed angelism face to the Nazi and fascist crimes.
-109 (average time of a Moon) John-Paul Ist (1978-1978). He died 33 days after his election.
-110 (labor of the Sun) John-Paul II (1978-2005). It is Fatima's sun working; It is the Holy Father who will achieve the Virgin's prophecy.

-112 (Peter the Roman). He is the first and the last pope: "In the last persecution of the Christian Church will sit Peter the Roman who will make his sheep graze through numerous tribulations. After these, the city with the seven hills (Rome) will be destroyed, and a formidable Judge will judge his people. The end."

Obviously, it is impossible for an author to elaborate such a long and precise list of all the popes, even for an inspired writer of the 11th or the 16th century. On the contrary, it is much easier to elaborate this list afterwards, especially for a well-known author, previous Jesuit priest in Rome from 1958 to 1964, like Malachi Brendan Martin (an Irishman again), who besides officially wrote the saga of the Popes, a prodigious fresco of the history of papacy from Saint Peter to John-Paul II. Therefore, we can think that the Irish Malachi Martin and not the Irish saint Malachi wrote the Prophecy of the popes.

We can wonder how his manuscript was found in Venice in 1595! There intervenes Gabriel, who "mails" himself the manuscript at the beginning of the 1590's, just with his machine to go back in time. The Benedictine monk Arnold de Wyon finds it "by chance" and publishes it in 1595. As soon as it is read, the manuscript belongs to our collective memory to the point of becoming an obvious reality inherited from the past. The hypothesis that such an amazingly precise premonitory text could have been written 400 years ago is particularly fantastic, although curiously admitted. It seems finally less fantastic, because more logical, that it could have been written after the facts it tells and "mailed" afterwards by a "chrononaut".

But Gabriel does not only takes advantage of our naivety when he makes us believe that a text from the 20th century is the work inspired by a saint from the 11th century, he also delivers us a message through the last pope of the prophecy, Peter the Roman, who will never exist but gives us a clue about the time when the Third World War started in the True History. It logically began with the invasion of the Franco-English Double Kingdom and of Italy, and particularly with the destruction of Rome (the city with seven hills) by the forces of the Warsaw Pact. It is during this last pontificate, not before and not after, that will happen the beginning of the Communist invasion, which was a prelude in the True History of the triggering of the nuclear war between North America and the Soviet Russia.

It is at the beginning of this war that they decided to send Gabriel into the past, leading a mixed team probably composed of four time travelers, for a desperate mission aiming at reversing the course of History by rewriting it from Antiquity on, because it is by attacking its roots that they could hope to modify it for a long time. We have described this secret mission all along this book, as well as we could according to the clues it had left us, underlining the exploit achieved by this American hero as discreet as prodigiously efficient. The technology he disposed of does not explain everything, he also needed intelligence, erudition, perseverance and an extraordinary sense of strategy in order to achieve his mission across the centuries and ensure the final triumph of his homeland against the inhuman totalitarianism, which had nearly destroyed it.

FALSE EPILOGUE

The future will say whether Gabriel Michael Santorum's story is the one of a stillborn little boy or the one, long and wonderful, that we have described in this book. The future will also say whether the United States will develop in the years 2040's a machine similar to the one used by Gabriel. If all this is confirmed, History will no longer be unique, but extended like in computing in several versions: The version 1.0 for the True History, the version 2.0 for the New History (the second one). The second, but maybe not the last one, because after Gabriel's death in 1996 occurred the air attack against the Twin Towers in Manhattan, on September 11, 2001. It is unlikely that the future President of the United States, having this new technology, will not use it to delete this national drama. He will thus have written the version 2.1 of History and we can imagine that there could be more of them afterwards, each time a catastrophe will not be avoided and that the security of the United States will be threatened. It could even become a method of governing, as the view of the immediate future of the actions on the battlefield could become a method of fighting. Remember the behavior of Joan of Arc during the Hundred Years War, which was in fact the first sample of the war of the future thanks to the introducing of this American technology, hidden behind the voices of the Saint.

Even if we consider that this story in only an ingenious tale (but who could swear to it without any risk?), was it right for the United States of today to reveal that the America of the first History has not only sent Jesus, Joan and Louis to execution, but made up the endless Franco-England wars in order to aim earlier at independence, and deliberately sent to death six million Jews, who should not even have been in the Europe occupied by the Nazis if Gabriel had not helped them to leave Egypt and later driven them to crucify a provocateur ? Of course it was in the praiseworthy aim to save the free world by driving as many wealthy or particularly educated Jews as possible towards America, in order to benefit from their forewarning genius and from their matchless scientific intuitions. But behind this sublime tribute, so expensive in human lives, how much unimaginable suffering! Beyond the memory of the Shoah, it seems to express itself now in the American collective unconscious by an unfailing support to the Hebrew State, as if to expiate Gabriel's fault.

John Richard Santorum.

Talking about the American presidential election, it is really strange that Senator Rick Santorum, the father of Gabriel Michael, hero of this book, was candidate to the Republican nomination to the election of November 6, 2012 and almost won the Primary? Does Gabriel use his father's political fame and the possible resort his father could be in case of the new administration's failure, in order to lead the Republican party into getting interested in his own mission through my tale? And finally, can the revelation that Senator Rick Santorum is an archangel's father and maybe Jesus's grandfather himself help him to be elected? Only Gabriel knows, for before he died in our History he saw the future and the answer to this crucial question.

THE LAW OF INERTIA

When I discovered the Apostolic Brief of Pope Pius XII, dated from a meaningful day for me, I started to feel that Gabriel might have been carrying on his mission for himself. The desperate mission that had been entrusted to him by the American President, chief of the Army very close to a military disaster, had been a complete success and should not go any further, condemned to oblivion. There comes Gabriel's ego: How to let people know about the extraordinary success of his secret mission, recognize his huge merit, even posthumously, and have it reflected upon his family?

There I intervened in my turn and I got the indirect proof of this through a series of violations of the law of inertia which rules, unlike what we feared, the trips in time and particularly in the past. These violations, even when they are only internal, need a considerable energy and thus a powerful and targeted intervention. They need the "force of God". I was given the demonstration of it through unexpected difficulties met by a person who is dear to me, to get over stages which our material means should have allowed to overfly easily. My first reaction was to rebel against the people apparently responsible for these difficulties. Then I realized that I cherished a woman who, without me, would have led a modest life and that this life might have been going on in the True History. Assuming that Gabriel had chosen her to help me accomplish my own mission in the New History, I was breaking the law of inertia at each kindness, without realizing it and trustfully. Hence those extremely rare incidents which regularly sabotaged my most sumptuous gifts.

The law of inertia also exists at a more general level. It explains the French exception, which means that France, even reduced to the Hexagon, strives to play a first-rate international role with reduced means and incredible cheek, which are taken at worst for arrogance or considered at best with surprise and friendliness. In fact, it is because Paris was in the True History the capital of the double Franco-English kingdom, and thus dominated half of the world. In the New History, the law of inertia wants Paris to take itself still for the most influent capital of the world, although it is only the most beautiful city in the world. The research presently led in Gramat, in the Lot department, on the French Z-machine pompously called Sphinx, show that France has not lost any of its pretentions.

The signing of the agreements at Lancaster House.

The Lancaster House agreements signed on November 2nd, 2010 between the French President and the United Kingdom's Prime Minister are another obvious manifestation of the law of inertia. The two blue-white-red flags get militarily closer in the house of Jean de Lancastre, regent of France better-known as the Duke of Bedford, who in the True History crossed the River Loire in Orleans, took Dauphin Charles prisoner and crowned young Henri VI, who had already been king of England since 1429, king of France in Reims cathedral in 1431. This way he inaugurated the long dynasty of the Double-Kingdom which, with its unique Franco-English army and the common Franco-Norman language, was going to dominate the world for such a long time. The military intervention in 2011 in Libya where both countries led together 80% of the airstrikes showed the perfect coordination of the two armies, the adaptability of the Rafale plane, but also the need to build a British aircraft carrier and to make a common drone. The Griffin Strike UK-French military exercise led by the new Combined Joint Expeditionary Force in April, 2016 in Wales confirmed that a 10,000 men Force is going to resuscitate in the short term the powerful Anglo-French Army of the True History. A common nuclear installation where the "performance of the nuclear heads will be modeled" was even decided in Valduc, in Burgundian territory, which reminds us of the alliance between the Duke of Burgundy and the Duke of Bedford during the Hundred Years War. This is the return by inertia of the powerful Anglo-French army of the True History, after the strategic parenthesis wanted by Gabriel in the New History in order to save Northern America from Soviet invasion.

The law of inertia also exists strangely in the assassination of President Kennedy; it is meaningful in the True History but reveals incomprehensible and useless in the New History, if we do not guess that it is a tragic manifestation of the law of inertia. It is also a strong   clue from the History that preceded us. Like the American survivalists' movement, which seems so absurd and ridiculous in our present History. However so many of them have converted their basement and dug an anti-atomic shelter in order to protect themselves from a nuclear "Armageddon". Born in the United States during the Cold War, at the time of the crisis of the Cuban missiles in October, 1962, this movement has not been unfailing since, in spite of the remoteness of the nuclear peril. It only takes all its meaning in the True History, in which the survivors of the Third World War which devastated Northern America were the provident Americans (today they are called the preppers, "those who get prepared") who organized their survival a long time before the years 2040's. Again an expression of the law of inertia!

This law of inertia and the temporal solution to the missing mass of the Universe (the insufficient mass of Universe finds its solution in the dimension of time which multiplies the mass of one to the other's every violation, the missing mass becoming a reserve mass) will anyway be the essential discoveries, with the spatial solutions of the missing genome (the telluric embryogenesis described by the French psychiatrist Méric) which are going to constitute the cultural revolution of the 21st century through three fundamental changes of paradigms.

Finally, it was when I discovered his father's surprise victory on January 4, 2012, in the Republican Primary, then in three more states on February 7, then in three other states on March 6, having nearly an equal score with his adversary in Ohio, then in two new states on March 13 and, on March 24, in the very symbolical state of Louisiana, that I understood that Gabriel had decided to try to have his father elected at the presidency of the United States of America. There too, he would break the law of temporal inertia for his father had undoubtedly never been elected in the True History (they would never have sent a President's son in such a perilous mission). Unless he had simply wanted to attract Obama's administration's attention over my book and so on his mission, through the political role played by his father. I also understood that his relatively young age (11 years less than his adversary) and the promise of a victorious Primary in 2015 led Santorum to leave the field open to Mitt Romney for the Republican nomination. Secondarily, I was less surprised that in France the embassy of the United States was established along Gabriel Avenue…

But there was another less reassuring hypothesis. Gabriel might have seen in the future, before he died, a new and serious threat for his own camp, which, most ironically, he would have created himself by altering history. His father would then have to sound the alarm in the American opinion, and to ward off this new danger by neutralizing it at its beginning. We think about the Ayatollahs' Iran if it took possession of the nuclear weapon and about its strategic Russian ally (here they are again!) not much more democratic under the reign of the FSB than under the communist party. Israel, which Gabriel also helped to create after having nearly exterminated its future population, is apparently looking forward to it. The taking over of the centrist party Kadima by General Mofaz on March 27, 2012, then his surprise alliance on May 8th with the Right party Likoud in power seem to confirm this intention. The arrival of a Jewish general born in Teheran (Who knows his enemy…) in a government of national union is in complete agreement with that direction.

Tsahal is ready to swoop down on the Iranian nuclear installations, especially since President Obama has decided to allow him to dispose of 4 more supply planes KC-135 and of anti-bunker GBU-31 bombs, which can be dropped from the bomber-fighter F15 from his army. The direct intervention of the US Air Force would however be necessary for the best protected Iranian target is the site of uranium enriching in Fordow, near the city of Qom, which has functioned since January 2012 and is buried under a mountain in which the rock can be 80 meters deep and even more, not mentioning the extra protection of concrete. For this, even the American bombs GBU-57 MOP (massive Ordnance Penetrator) of more than 13.5 tons will not be enough, because they only penetrate 60 meters in the ground before exploding. So we had to rely upon the statements of the Secretary of Defense, Leon Panetta, who asserted that the American army will receive a modernized version of "bunker buster bomb" able to destroy the deepest underground shelters. Then the American Air Force would be the only one able to carry such heavy bombs, thanks to its B-2 or B-52 bombers.

The political aim to use these weapons for a strategic and preventive purpose remained to be demonstrated. We could doubt about it when we learned that John Kerry, the chief of American diplomacy in Obama's administration 2, was a well-known sceptic as far as military interventionism was concerned, after having been a pacifist militant when he came back from the Vietnam War. Moreover, his daughter Vanessa was married to Beyrouz Vala Naheed, a doctor or Iranian origin who had family in the Islamic Republic and was still going to Tehran to visit its members. As many potential hostages who could have hung over the Secretary of State's decisions! Yet John Kerry's grandparents on his father's side were Austrian Jews, but Fritz Köhn had changed his name into Kerry and converted to Catholicism in 1901.

We can finally wonder whether the resignation three days after Obama's reelection of the four-star General David Petraeus, the much respected director of the CIA, was not an essential pre-condition to John Kerry's nomination at the head of the Department of State. The appointment of Chuck Hagel, declared sworn enemy of the pro-Israeli lobby at the Congress, as successor of Leon Panetta as Secretary of Defense was truly linked with more precise and oriented logic.

But in the Middle East, till the necessary American-Israeli intervention, the way was open for the Iranians, whatever may be the economic sanctions or the deceitful nuclear deal, to enrich their uranium and obtain nuclear weapons thanks to the famous *taqiyya*, which allows Muslims to lie to unbelievers in order to defeat them (Qur'an 16:106). The countdown of a second and useless holocaust had begun…

THE RESERVE MASS

We have to come back for a short while to the temporal solution of the missing mass of the Universe, which we referred to in the previous chapter. The reader who is not keen on exact sciences or not really fond of speculation in that field will advantageously be able to jump over this chapter and go straight on to the following one.

The astrophysicists teach us that the stars situated at the periphery of the spiral galaxies, like the Sun in the Milky Way, turn much too rapidly around the center of the galaxies, and so their orbital velocity are not only determined by the gravitational attraction of all the observable stars. Newton's laws of gravitation indicate that these galaxies should contain much more matter than the one we are able to observe. This invisible matter is called dark matter, for it can only be detected through its gravitational field. We are even taught that this dark matter should represent 90% of the whole mass of the Universe.

Still, Einstein explains the gravitational force as the curving of a four-dimensioned time-space (theory of general relativity). So we understand that the enormous mass of the dark matter will curve the space of the galaxy until the speed of rotation of the surrounding stars around its center is accelerated. It will also attract the time (which becomes curved in its turn), for space and time are inextricably linked. Besides, we can wonder whether the dark matter is not visible at the present because it would be attracted by the curving of time in an unobservable past. The visible stellar matter would be like the tip of an iceberg, of which the greatest part would become immersed into the depths of the ocean of time. When you know that 90% of the volume of an iceberg is situated under the surface of water, the comparison is striking.

The iceberg's theory.

We often forget that the reverse is true and that the curving of time (a trip backwards) will attract space with itself. This is what happens when Gabriel travels back 3,500 years into the past of a Universe whose age is estimated at 14 billion years. He attracts with himself all the space of the Universe during his trip back in time. And then, according to the law of conservation of energy (or its mass equivalent), he borrows from the dark matter, which becomes a reserve mass we can explain this way:

$$M^{tot} = 100$$
$$M^{res} = 90 = \frac{x.V^{ref}}{U^{ref}} = \frac{x.3.5}{14,000,000} = \frac{x}{4,000,000}$$
$$x = 90 . 4,000,000 = 360,000,000$$

M^{tot} = Total mass of the Universe

M^{res} = Reserve mass

V^{ref} = Reference trip (3,500 years)

U^{ref} = Reference age of the Universe (14 billion years)

We can see from this equation that Gabriel's trip back in time only gives a little scrape into the mass reserve. However, the total number of reference trips is not infinite, but limited to 360 million for all the civilizations able to achieve this exploit in the Universe. Eventually, we can see that the law of temporal inertia has its source in the reserve mass, for any mass is defined by its inertia in the space which we have to master in order to move it. So the time not only has a shape (curved) but also a mass (inertia).

If we compare our equation to Einstein-Grossmann's, in which the curving G is proportional to the mass T:

$$G_{ij} = \frac{8\pi G}{C^4} \cdot T_{ij}$$

We notice that if the reserve mass is opened by a trip in time, and so diminishes, the curving diminishes proportionally to the mass, so the speed of rotation of the outlying stars around the center of the galaxy diminishes. If we can measure the variations of this speed over the ages by measuring it on various distances on stars, whose light comes from various eras (the Sun's takes 8' to reach us), we shall be able to check the reduction of this speed and deduce that one or several civilizations in the Milky Way, including ours, have carried out trips in time.

THE THREAT

In the Christian Occident, the Church is clearly separate from the State. In Iran, as in all the Muslim countries (except Turkey), the spiritual power is mingled with the temporal power. Gabriel wanted it so to create a counter power, factor of progress, in the Christian countries: It is the Occidental model, also adopted by the modern Buddhist countries. He enforces, after having for a long time prevented the Jews from going back to Palestine, a hidden superiority to Christendom, but which can prove to be dangerous as soon as a Muslim country has access to the atomic weapon. For Pakistan, the counter power is exerted by the Indian neighbor, who is also nuclearized. For Iran, the counter power is no more exerted by the Soviet bear, reduced in 1990 to the Russian teddy bear, and the access to the atomic weapon will give the Ayatollah Khamenei, supreme Guide of the Islamic Revolution, the means to annihilate the Jewish and Europeans misbelievers. All the more as he now profits from missiles with a 1180 miles range, which can thus reach Israel or the Eastern Europe.

In Europe, the American bases are protected by antimissile ships of Aegis class which sail about in the Mediterranean Sea, but only the French Air Force has had since November 2011 an operational ground-to-air system of intermediate terrestrial range called Mamba, equipped with Aster antimissile missiles able to intercept ballistic missiles of Scud type within a radius of 190 miles. Five French aircraft bases will be progressively equipped. Israel is also equipped with an antimissile system with, more particularly, which would be the best anti-missile in the world, the Arrow 3, intended to intercept the Iranian missile Shahab-3 which has a range of 800 miles and can be provided with a conventional head of 760 to 1,100 kilos.

THE COUNTER-ATTACK

Thanks to the success of Gabriel's mission, America, in the New History, lives in perfect bliss. It dominates the economical and financial world, it is the first technological and military power, it is the police of the planet. As always, when everything goes particularly well, people do not wonder about it. The Russians were wondering, though. Why such unbalance, such delay on the American rival, although themselves had been so close to dominate the world ? The Russian president Vladimir Poutine, previous colonel of the KGB, even declared in front of the Parliament on April 26, 2005, that "the disappearance of the USSR was the greatest geopolitical catastrophe of the twentieth century". Besides, he has restored the old national anthem, the red flag for the military units, and lately, the title of "Hero of work" in the factories : They call this "nostalinalgia".

All this shows especially that the Russians still do not understand how the catastrophe happened : this book brings them an unexpected element of answer. The economical failure of communism does not explain everything, especially since the fall of Berlin's Wall. And as the Kremlin will always remain the Kremlin, and that the FSB is the KGB's daughter, the Russians made use of their spying services.

The Americans themselves were soon going to give them the opportunity of entering the core of their triumphant technology. In the climate of post-communist easing and of generalized world-wide spreading, they appealed without much mistrust to the electronic Institute of high intensity currents in Tomsk, in Russia, because they needed their Linear Transformer Driver generator in order to maintain every ten seconds the process of fusion by inertial confinement of the Z-machine. The fast-repeating shoots were actually necessary for the future centrals to produce an unlimited electrical energy from sea water, which is abundant and cheap. The Americans had the internal combustion engine, the Russians would supply with the cylinders in order to make an over-powerful and economical V12.

The LTD generator in Tomsk (Siberia).

The Sandia laboratory, in Albuquerque (New Mexico), is part of the National nuclear Security Administration. Obsessed by the revolutionary success that they felt within reach, the Americans only neglected one word: Security. Yet U.S. Intelligence should remember Aesop's fable, The Eagle and the Arrow, whose symbols are contained on the frontside of the U.S. Seal. An eagle flying in the sky is shot by an arrow. Before dying, it realizes that the arrow has been feathered with one of its own plumes. Moral: Let us not give our enemy the mean for our own destruction!

The Antonov freight planes started to discharge the Russian generators with ultra-short impulsion on Albuquerque airport in order to replace the enormous isolating pool full of water and the power switches of the American Z-machine. But, at the same time, the first Russians technicians, who were indispensable to look after those complex devices, arrived. One of them had to mix into the Russo-American team and to get married, found a family and succeed in his job, without ever getting in touch with the services that had sent him. His long-term mission was to remain unnoticed.

Boris, so we shall call him, will take part at the beginning of the 2040's in the first industrial applications of the Z-machine. One of them will particularly catch his attention for its strategic applications. It consisted of the attempts to go through the light barrier under very high energy, with the clear aim to hope to travel back in time. He took part in the first experiments of sending material objects, which necessarily were to precede the sending of animal or human material. Boris was so well introduced in the team and he spoke English so well that everybody had forgotten that he had only been naturalized through marriage.

When the making of parameters became more precise, and the animal experiments began, Boris naturally suggested his own dog, Tom, asserting that the animal trusted him, which would let him avoid stress during the experience. Boris had carefully kept the same residence, and he still lived in the same house in a wealthy area of Los Alamos, where his children had comfortably grown up. His plan was that the dog would find it easily when he would be propelled into the past and land at the beginning of the 2020's. This jump of about twenty years had seemed enough to the experts for a first experience and Boris had insisted on it, so that the dog should not run too much risk.

Tom left for his trip with his usual collar on, under his master's reassuring eyes. What nobody knew, is that Boris had hidden in his collar a memory card from the 2020's, which could easily be read by the computers from those years. In it, he had registered (with an old PC that he kept religiously) all the strategic information he had collected, and, in particular, the success of a science-fiction book published in the United States. This book had contributed to Santorum's election as a president of the United States, and so had broken the geopolitical balance in the Middle East, to the prejudice of Russia and its Shiite allies.

When Tom landed in the past, he did not feel lost very long, and his instinct led him to the house he had always known. In fact, Boris heard a dog scratching at the door, he did not know it but the dog jumped over him, wagging his tail freneti-cally. He was wearing grotesque dark glasses, which actually had protected his eyes from the hyper-intense flash when he crossed the light barrier. Boris noticed the animal's collar and soon found the memory card he had sent to himself twenty years later. Less than a week later, Tom's card was flying towards Tomsk on the first plane leaving for the Siberian institute.

The Russian secret services reacted immediately and desperately tried to prevent the publishing of this book, of which incomplete printings were already circulating, particularly at the French editors. They had to act discreetly in order not to compromise their precious agent from the future. So they chose to wake up a sleeping agent, as Gabriel had awoken one to come and help me in my life, and as the French story-teller Perrault had done in The Sleeping Beauty.

You can recognize a sleeping agent in the fact that it is a beautiful, middle-aged woman, who vegetates unaccountably in her life, professionally underestimated, free from any engagement, and who unexpectedly benefits of an extraordinary combination of circumstances. My own wife, before I realized the mission I had been attributed, left me in a few months for a strong woman with heavy curves and a precarious situation, without much instruction, whom I found subjectively ugly and arrogant. Even if she satisfied in this affair so far unexpressed pulsions, the seriousness and application which she destroyed our little family with, were properly speaking amazing. In a word, the most unlikely scenario, the absolute miracle.

The miracle was confirmed when Gabriel introduced me, a little while later, because time counted, the discreetly off-the-wall woman, who was full of cautious sensuality, of class, of education, of intelligence, elegance, and, most important, jealous of her territory, and who was going to help me so efficiently in my mission. A jewel waiting for its jewel-case ! With her, I started a dual creative system, which I had cruelly missed so far, and which increased spectacularly my intellectual production. Eventually, I took so much her constructive criticism into account that I will not reveal everything to the reader in order to ensure our own security, and I will keep essential information to myself, for they touch me personally. Revealing secrets concerning the security of the United States, keeping others about the informer and change him into a secret agent, had not history been a long spy novel since the end of prehistory ?

My new wife also brought me insistent signals about which I finally recognized that they were addressed to me through her. I was puzzled because my wife, although she was perfectly dark-haired and hated all the blond-haired women, unconditionally admired Marilyn Monroe, a woman both fragile and influential, and especially the model of the sensual without vulgarity woman. She was literally fascinated by Marilyn's magic, by her animal beauty, for her she was a timeless icon and actually she was right. The house was filled with books, magazines and calendars about Marilyn, so that we owned a whole collection. The hypothesis of her assassination in the night of the 4th of August, 1962, did not seem unlikely to me, but I found it difficult to understand how a man could have ordered to kill a sex-symbol like Marilyn. So I applied the old saying of the police : search for the woman !

I had kept in memory the famous Happy birthday, Mr Pres-ident sung by Marilyn on May 19, 1962 at the Madison Square Garden, with such a sensual voice that the numerous spectators had no doubt about the nature of her relationship with President Kennedy. Marilyn, who had not been legally recognized by her biological father, did not rest until she was recognized by all the population, but also by the nation's father, that is to say the Presi-dent himself, a man otherwise quite handsome. Jackie Kennedy's death on a 19th of May (1994) shows that her emotional life had stopped on that day, which was exceedingly harmful in the life of a loving, unfairly ridiculed woman.

After such a public humiliation, I imagined the legitimate reaction of (the dark-haired) Jackie Kennedy and it had to be what had really happened in the True History. The couple's conflict had burst out publicly after the scandal and Jackie sued for a divorce during the Summer 1962. The bleached-haired star marries then the president, who manages disastrously the crisis of Cuba, and the Cold War goes up a step. So she will be the one who will get Kennedy's brain on the boot of the Lincoln on November 23, 1963 in Dallas (her first gore part). From these events on, all wives of the candidates to the presidency (except Michelle Obama) will be platinum blondes, in order to imitate Marilyn and match the new standards of seduction.

In the New History, Gabriel knows that there is not a woman but a very influential homosexual whose interest is to have Marilyn assassinated, for he considers her as a threat to national security. It is the almighty FBI director, Edgar Hoover, who does not like women, and especially those who try to entice the president from his duty in the core of an international crisis. So the Summer 1962 will be the Summer of her true-false suicide and not the one of her short triumph. At the same time, Gabriel points out that my wife has actually been sent to me, because she brings this incongruous message, which obsesses her although she cannot explain it herself. As a privilege usually reserved to the chiefs of state, Hoover will have state funerals when he dies in 1972.

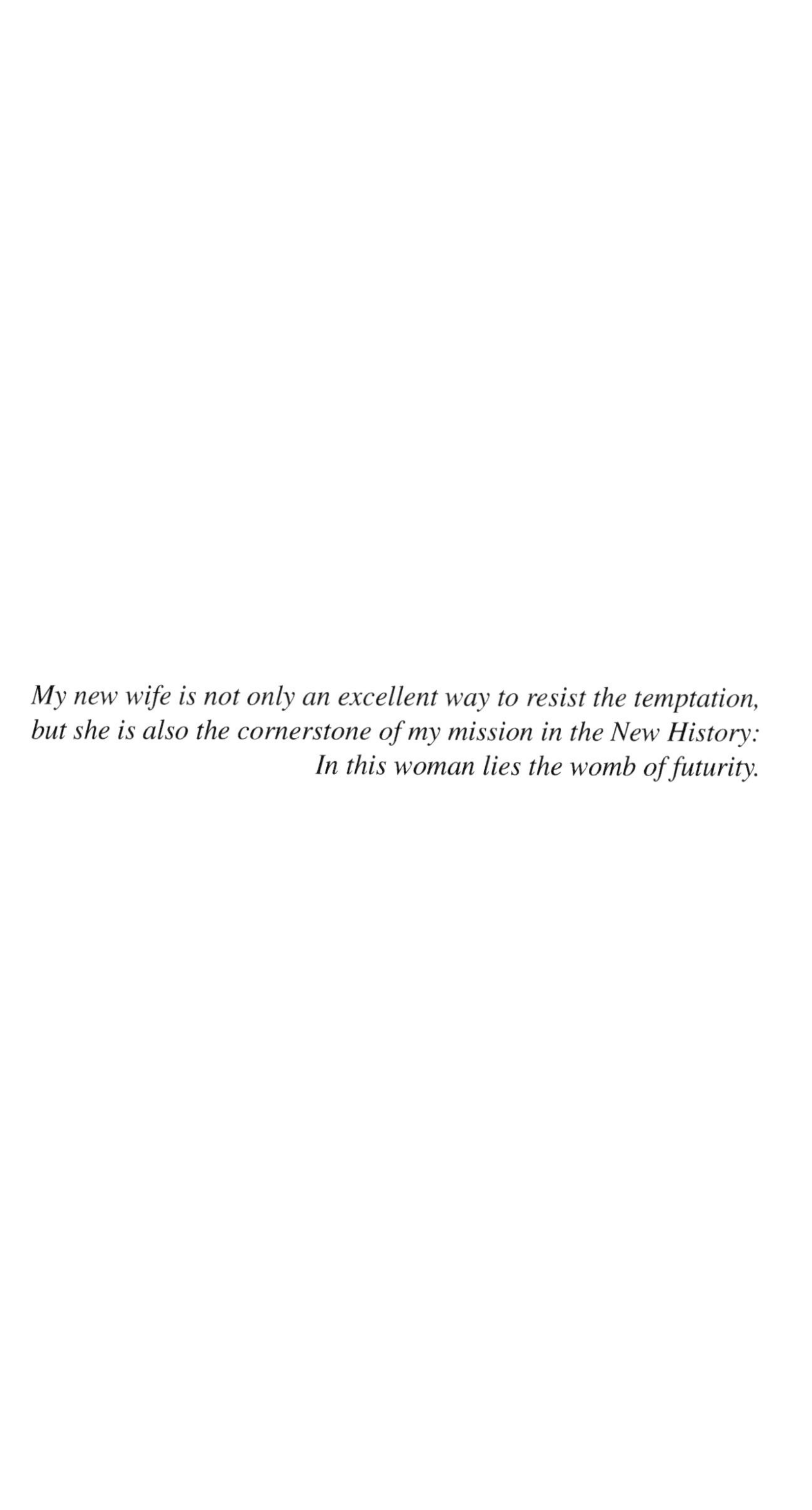

My new wife is not only an excellent way to resist the temptation,
but she is also the cornerstone of my mission in the New History:
In this woman lies the womb of futurity.

THE TEMPTATION

The Russians also tried to entice me from my mission. By a mere chance I came across the beautiful Natasha's way. Younger of course than my own wife, taller, blonde, from a modest condition but full of natural class, with a wonderful smile, I had to admit that Russians had not mocked at me: they had sent me a supermodel. She had just been left abruptly by her companion and complained bitterly. I thought that her companion was really particular, and I was on my guard, because I had already lived the same unlikely situation. I knew that, in the True History, the Soviets had scattered in the free world sleeping agents, who, in the New History, did not remember the role they had to play, but remained programmed by the law of temporal inertia.

It was confirmed one day when Natasha was surprised because some Russians had talked to her several times in their own language during her holidays on the Azure Coast in France. On this occasion she remembered that she had a Russian grandfather, and to my opinion, the look of a Bolshoi ballet dancer that matched. Her attempts at seducing were diverse but unconscious, because she remained deeply attached to her companion who had run away. Sometimes she wore provocative outfit: high-heeled boots or shoes that made her silhouette more interminable, too shorts skirts which forced her to pull on them when she crossed her legs. Sometimes she referred to a friend who had a relationship with a married man, to a trip she had to give up because she had no money and that I could easily afford to pay, sometimes there was a glimmer of interest in her eyes when she mistook the meaning of a compliment, and sometimes a remark about her love of good books I naturally shared. But she persisted in trying to understand why the man she loved had left her, and she even managed to make him come back to her to justify himself. He expressed sincere regrets and even offered her a ring, unfortunately too big for her long slender fingers. Then she gave up all their projects, suddenly defiant and resigned.

I could not tell her that she was a victim of the law of temporal inertia and that in the True History her matrimonial projects were accomplished, that she got married, she had a child and she probably put on weight (which was shown by the too large ring). Then she had given up this relationship herself, because she had to choose between her child and an exclusive and jealous companion, who could not bear to share her love with another person. But in the New History, she was condemned to play her role as a sleeping agent and to try to achieve the mission for which she had been awakened.

Gabriel had chosen me because he knew that I would be able to manage that kind of situation. I found nevertheless that I had merit. So I kept Natasha at a distance, even if I felt that she was attracted and unconsciously willing to accomplish her secret mission, that is to say turn me away from mine with the sweetest of traps. However I was all the time haunted by a possible less discreet sabotage of the aims I had assigned to myself, by a less subtle counter-attack which would put an end to months of analysis and reconstitution of the past. What had Gabriel foreseen in such circumstances? Could he protect me till the end?

If you are American and you read this book, it means that I will have finally accomplished my mission, with the quasi-divine help of Gabriel.

Gabriel is the Eternal for he travels in time and gives the impression that he is eternal.

Santorum is the Saint of Saints, who made the Santorin collapse in order to lead the Hebrews out of Egypt.

Gabriel is the Eternal who crossed times for the triumph of the country he finally sanctuarized.

This country is the land of the First Amendment, the country of the liberty of expression, the real Savior of the world !

The Constitution of the U. S. A. (First Amendment).

IN GOD WE TRUST

Barack Obama was a good (and handsome) President. I am in great respect of his domestic policy: in particular, he has succeeded in revolutionizing the health care system and America is still the world's leading economy and military power. However, his foreign policy was nearly a disaster. Despite he is the man who got Osama bin Laden, he has actually committed two big mistakes. The first mistake occurred in his first term, after the fraudulent Iranian presidential election in 2009, when he did not try to help the millions of protesters who fought in the streets of many Iranian cities against the wild repression by the Basij, subordinate to the Islamic revolution Guardians and the Supreme leader Ayatollah Khamenei. The second mistake occurred in his second term when he signed on November 24, 2013 the Geneva Agreement on the Iranian nuclear program, although the French Foreign Minister Laurent Fabius was reluctant. This reminds us of the Munich Agreements in 1938 between Hitler, Chamberlain and Daladier. They believed that they were saving the peace, but they eventually precipitated World War II. "You have chosen dishonor and you will get war", Winston Churchill could have told Barack Obama. History is repeating itself.

Kkamenei has played Obama for a fool, dispatching his Western-educated, English-fluent Foreign Minister Zarif to charm him, as Hitler dispatched his Western-educated, former Pommery champagne salesman, English and French-fluent Foreign Minister von Ribbentrop to charm his future enemies. History is repeating itself. The problem is that Obama is a lawyer and not a military chief. He desperately wants to avoid the prospect of military action and meanwhile he underestimated the perversity of the Iranian regime.

John Kerry could have become a good President. The problem is that Kerry is not a military chief either. Electing him would mean a disaster for Israel and maybe even for a large part of Europe. In fact, with Obama and Kerry, the fate of the future Iranian nuclear threat remained unclear.

Senator Richard Santorum seems to be the sole leader able to deal with the crisis and to avoid both a huge slaughter in Israel (a real new holocaust) and bringing shame on America. He must finish his son's job and save the world from a dreadful danger. Imagine nuclear weapons in Hitler's hands! Santorum's election will be the clincher, because he perfectly knows that the new foe is the true woe and must be remorselessly destroyed.

Gabriel's mission will only be achieved if his father finds, in time, the necessary means to erase radically the nuclear capacity of a country that is reportedly managed by a paranoiac

Ayatollah, whose own "Mein Kampf" comes down to "Death to America and to Israel". The Presidential campaign of 2016 (or at the latest that of 2020) will be the most crucial political contest in American history, after the campaign of 1864 (Lincoln v. McClellan), because the stakes will be to avoid the first nuclear regional war and for United States to keep the strategic leadership of the world.

Contrary to Ian Bremmer, president of a political-risk consultancy, Gabriel obviously "refuses to accept anything short of Iran's total surrender" (*Time* June 15, 2015), like the German's total surrender in other times but for the same reason (the supreme leader's paranoia). Washington should continue to focus on upcoming Iran's nukes, because they are massive destruction weapons and because Iran's supreme leader probably wants to build them in order to use them, not to deter Israel from using its own. Even if Washington and Moscow miraculously avoided the use of nuclear weapons during the Cold War, the "Mein Kampf" rhetoric from the Ayatollah Khamenei leads to believe he is really suicidal.

Hillary Clinton's case is something different. Progressive Democrats tend to see her as a hawk in foreign affairs and they are right: She is a robust proponent of military intervention and has more balls than most male candidates have. For a long time she has shown a strong appetite for the race and she is ready to challenge anybody in the general election. However, before he died, Gabriel foresaw that Hillary Clinton would not be able to smash the glass ceiling and would not become the first female President of the United States.

All these men and woman are alumni of America's original college town (Boston) : Obama (Harvard), Kerry (Boston College) and Clinton (Wellesley College). Israeli Prime Minister Netanyahu, although he has also graduated in Boston (MIT), becomes conscious that Boston's superior universitary status is a fake, that all these Boston graduates have failed in politics about his own country and that he could expect more from another college town: why not Pittsburgh (Santorum) or even Philadelphia (Trump)?

In case of the Republican's failure, we will still remain under threat from the future President of the United States in the 2040's who could then decide to reverse the result of Florida's election in 2000 and give the victory to Al Gore. Anyway, this one would have won the election without the fraud which occurred whereas Jeb Bush (George W. Bush's brother) was the Governor of this State. Bush won by a razor-thin margin of only 537 votes out of almost 6 million cast! Good news for the climate and for Saddam Hussein, because Al Gore –the ecologist– would never have invaded Iraq after September 11, 2001 and Khamenei in Iran would not have benefitted of this stupid invasion. By writing this 2.1 version of History, which will erase the version we are living, the future President will restore by this way the necessary balance between Sunnis and Shiites in the Middle East.

America may really trust God, because God in fact is American.

INSIDER DEALING

In May 2011, Donald Trump bowed out before Republican nomination in 2012 for the White House race. Then apparently most of his supporters decided to vote for Richard Santorum. In 2015, Trump did not only promote the Donald. He was really eager to become respectable (after becoming a billionaire) and did not give up the race, in spite of the Federal Electoral Commission regulations. In 2016, he won the Republican nomination in a landslide, partly because of the numerous contenders who scattered the Republican votes. Unlike Santorum, it would be noted that Trump talks to the people with short, simple, hardhitting sentences that he repeats many times like slogans or ads, with the hypnotic effect peculiar to populist leaders, so that he is easier to understand than Santorum for the lower class.

Meanwhile, in the Far East of Europe, President Obama was leading a policy worthy of a Peace Nobel Price, avoiding waging a military war against the asymmetric war led in Ukraine by the crafty Russian President. A wise policy indeed because this New Cold War was only the expression of the law of temporal inertia, that is to say of the "hostile coexistence" (without Detente) which ruled at that time in the True History and led to World War III in the early 2040's. President Putin was crafty because he had invaded Ukraine only to negotiate in a strong position the annexation of Crimea, which in fact was not an historical crime.

Instead of carrying on a risky military war, President Obama was carrying on a devastating economic war against Russia, which–added to the collapse of the oil price–was seriously weakening its economy. In order to break the diplomatic deadlock, the two nations had obviously to negotiate and, to understand that, we must go back into the past–the true past and the new past… Remember! In the True History, America is surrounded by the Soviet missiles from Cuba and California and Alaska, and about to surrender or die, till the American President sends Gabriel back into the past to fix the history. In the New History, the rivalry between the religions of the Book he had himself created indirectly led to the Crimean War, the capture of Sebastopol by the French and British Armies and the ruin of Russia: £144 million spent in this war from 1852 to 1856. Thus all began in Crimea and all will also end in Crimea…

A few years earlier, at the end of 1841, John Sutter bought Fort Ross $30,000 from the Russians. But Sutter was a Mexican citizen; therefore Fort Ross and the land around became Mexican. On January 24, 1848, gold was discovered in the vicinity of Sutter's Mill: The gold rush was beginning. On February 2, 1848, only nine days after the discovery, which was not known yet by the "forty-niners"–the overwhelming number of gold-seekers who came to California in 1849–the treaty of

Guadeloupe Hidalgo gave California to USA. The gold fields became property of the US government. One can speculate that if Tsar Nicholas I had known that so much gold ($25.8 billion at the end of the 19th century) would be discovered forty miles east of Fort Ross, he would never have approved the sale. He would rather have sent soldiers to North California. What an unlucky Tsar indeed!

On March 30, 1867 again, another Tsar – Alexander II – will be still more unlucky when he decides to sell Alaska to the United States, just after the American Civil War. The "Seward's folly" – Seward was Lincoln's Secretary of State – did not turn out to be so foolish since the purchase of $7.2 million ($121 million today) will yield $1 billion ($16.8 billion today) after the discovery of a major gold deposit in the Klondike (Yukon River) in 1896, then in Nome (mouth of the Yukon River) in 1899. The treaty was signed just three months before Canadian Confederation was realized, in July 1867. In fact, the Dominion of Canada could have welcomed Alaska like British Columbia into the confederation in 1871. The transfer ceremony took place in New Archangel (so called in honour of Saint Michael) on October 18, 1867. But, when the Russian flag, which looks like the modern Californian flag, had to be pulled down to give way to the flag of the United States, it got surprisingly entangled at the top of the spar. This is obviously another expression of the law of temporal inertia, for the Russian flag had never been pulled down in the True History.

Finally, the United States earned by chance $42.5 billion (not to mention the interests) and literally stole two strategic states from Russia in less than half a century. Of course Americans in 1841 and 1867 could not have foreseen and known what the financial return of North California and Alaska purchases would be. Except if an American time traveler, who knew for certain that such quantities of gold would be found in those countries in 1848 and 1896, prompted them in secret to make a deal before. If it is confirmed in a near future, it will be the first and most important insider dealing throughout the history!

When President Putin realizes that Russia has really been fucked by a cheating America and claims the restitution of the $42.5 billion in front of a federal court, what American will be the most capable to stand up to him if it is not the actual time traveler's father? Unfortunately, it turned out that Santorum could not win the Republican primary in front of Trump and he decided as early as February 2nd to suspend his 2016 GOP primary campaign.

When Trump surprisingly won the general election, it became obvious that the glass ceiling prevented Ms. Clinton from being the first female President in the US history and that Trump's campaign slogan "Make America great again" was in fact "Make America white again" and even "English again". In England, Brexit was the revenge of the Hastings battle (1066), the revenge of the English people who speak a poor everyday language from German descent against the Norman elites who speak a rich and civilized English from French and Latin descent. You see the same division between the House of Lords and the House of Commons: The Lords are the landlords of the ground, that is to say the heirs of the Norman barons to whom William the Conqueror distributed the land he had conquered; The Commons are the common people who were defeated, dispossessed of the land by the continental invaders and did not even know writing at that time. And worse, U.K. carried out itself in

2016–because of the future steep tariffs on monthly exports of more than $15 billion to E.U. nations–the Continental Blockade decided by Napoleon in 1806 and never achieved. Even a new Napoleon came back in France through the victory of Macron at the presidential election in 2017 and England will soon have to return to Brussels to stop his triumphal march in the land of Waterloo. Otherwise, Waterloo Station and Trafalgar Square will have to be piteously renamed Calais Station and Channel Square: Engels without Normans will be losers again. Similarly, on the other side of Atlantic Ocean, one could say that the 'Clintexit' was the revenge of the English people from the Midwest and the traditional belts (Rust belt, Bible belt) against the Norman elites composed of well-educated people from the West and North-East Coasts.

It appeared soon that Trump was not elected by chance (even if his victory was so narrow that Clinton gathered nearly 3 million votes more than him–the largest total ever for a losing candidate) and that Clinton was not sacrificed in vain. Indeed, Donald Trump's grandfather – Friedrich Trump – left the German small town of Kallstadt in 1885 for New York City. When the Gold Rush occurred in 1896, he traveled to Alaska where he set up some brothels and became wealthy. His son Frederick invested the fortune in real estate–mostly in New York especially in Queens and Brooklyn–with his German mother, but told after World War II that Trump's family was from Swedish origin because it was not a good thing for business to be German in the most Jewish city in the world. He even became friends with Benjamin Netanyahu, the future Prime Minister of Israel, who was then working in Manhattan for the UN. His son Donald just developed the business and crossed the East River to erect in Manhattan his own phallus tower which lastly seduced the beautiful

Melania, after many other women whom he mostly considered as the prostitutes hired by his grand-father. His own son-in-law, married to his favorite daughter, is a Jew and Ivanka even converted to Judaism in 2009. The hyper-Zionist Jared Kushner is today not only a senior adviser to the President, but he is also the fulcrum between the Oval office and Tel Aviv.

The most important, in our interpretation grid, is that Trump has become Russian in the True History and became American only in the New History, which–as we remember–was severely rigged thanks to the efforts of Gabriel Michael Santorum. There are two consequences: That means that Gabriel wanted absolutely Trump to become American–this is the third reason for the purchase of Alaska after its gold fields and its strategic position–and at the opposite that explains Trump's tropism for Russia by the law of temporal inertia. He likes Russia because he was a Russian citizen in the previous history. Notably he married two Slavic women (Ivana and Melania), he praises openly Russian President Vladimir Putin; He also said on July 27, 2016 that he hoped the Russians had hacked Clinton's emails and encouraged them to publish her private messages. It was the first time in the U.S. history that a future President could have been accused of 'foreign intelligence'. But unconsciously, because of the law of temporal inertia, it is only 'domestic intelligence' for him. Surprisingly, he appointed Rex Tillerson (T.rex in short vs. true predator like Putinnosaurus rex) as Secretary of State because he had strong ties with Russia as former Exxon's CEO. In the same way, he did not agree with Donald Tusk, president of the European Council, who should symbolically represent the NATO's 'tusks' for the GOP's elephant, because he knows he must instead strike a deal with Russia (against Iran and the last communist Asiatic countries) to prevent or delay what some centrist and left-leaning folks expect and fear as a 'Trumpocalypse'.

The next question is: Why did Gabriel want Trump to become the President-elect? The answer arose immediately from the significant nomination of the retired Marine Corps four-star General James Mattis as the Secretary of Defense on December 1, 2016, who therefore became a statutory attendee at the National Security Council. Mattis said in 2012, before he retired in 2013, that the three most serious threats facing the U.S. were "Iran, Iran, Iran." He is right if you understand "Iran in Iraq, Iran in Syria, and Iran in Lebanon." Great Iran is a nightmare not only for the U.S. but also for Saudi Arabia, for Israel, for Turkey, for Russia. Mattis's Iran intense antagonism has its genesis in a longstanding grievance, one that goes back to 1983 when 241 American soldiers, including 220 Marines, were killed by an Iran-trained suicide truck bomber in Beirut. That even led President Obama to replace him at the Head of the U.S. Central Command. He now takes revenge by controlling the Pentagon and finally indulging his old hate of the Islamic Republic.

Another significant nomination is the unexpected one (because illegal according to Title 50 of the U.S. Code, Section 3021) of Trump's chief strategist Stephen Bannon on January 28, 2017 as a regular attendee at the National Security Council. Indeed, as a junior officer on a US Navy destroyer he met on 1980 the USS Nimitz in the Gulf of Oman, just before the aircraft carrier launched helicopters, to rescue 52 U.S. Embassy hostages held in Tehran. But the mission failed because of a crash between two helicopters and the failed hostage rescue provided him with a sorry example of failed presidential leadership. This is why he chose to serve next-President Trump because he was at the exact opposite of then-President Carter, whose lack of leadership led him later to return Mar-a-Lago estate–Palm Beach, Fla.–to the Post family for sale and finally allowed Trump to buy it for only $8 million (Art of the Deal?).

Like Lt. Gen. Michael Flynn who had to resign as National Security Advisor on Feb. 13, 2017, Bannon is known as an Islamophobic. He appears to be an Iranophobic as well, a fierce adversary of the international nuclear deal with Iran and eager for a military confrontation with this country. Lt. Gen. H.R. McMaster who replaced Flynn at the National Security Council on Feb. 20, 2017 is a respected military strategist, but not an ideologue like Flynn or a political strategist like Bannon, thus not a rival for him. At first placed at the Council in order to control Flynn, he was no longer needed in that role, so a presidential memorandum removed him on April 4, 2017 from NSC's Principal's Committee. In fact, there are strong signs that Bannon became a true éminence grise as soon as the sole rival he had around the President was missing in action, thanks to the leaks of the FBI to the press about an investigation ordered by Obama: what a side effect!

But the military-minded Big Four Generals (Mattis, McMaster, Kelly, Dunford) succeeded in limiting Bannon's influence about National Security because their military strategy collided with his political strategy. Eventually, John Kelly as new White House Chief of Staff removed him from the White House on August 18, 2017. It looked like a military coup, not against the President but against the ungovernable factional feuding around the President among generals led by McMaster, relatives led by Kushner and populists led by Bannon. With a West Wing almost under martial law, Trump seemed steady for the first time in six months and, backed both by the Marine Corps and the Jewish Corporation ("Javanka" and Cohn), now invincible.

Trump is an actor who is attracted by disruptive men and paranoid personalities (Flynn, Bannon) who direct him by giving him disruptive scenarios to play. But Trump defers also to the military brass, because he was impressed by the New York Military Academy he enrolled in at age 13 for five years and he likes guys with a killer instinct. I quote General Mattis himself: "Be polite, be professional, but have a plan to kill everyone you meet." Among the first military implementations of his term, there is the biggest U.S. military budget increase–by $54bn– since Irak war he asked Congress in his first budget proposal on March 2, 2017, including the increase of the Marine Corps to 36 battalions from 23 which is the Mattis's personal touch, that likely announces–after ISIS' defeat–a future large attack against Iran and its nuclear facilities. In short, the main features of this mercurial man in the Oval Office are his natural petulance and his 'Apprentice' personality: prone to exaggeration, inclination to hyperbole, with a colloquial speech and very ostentatious words. His broken syntax and unclear comments are those of a foreign speaker and remind of his Russian origin in the True History.

Incidentally or not, many other nominations were in the wake of that of Jared Kushner, his Jewish son-in-law: Friedmann, a long time Trump's attorney who speaks Hebrew perfectly, as US ambassador to Israel; Mnuchin, a former Goldman Sachs executive, as Treasury secretary; Cohn, an outgoing COO at Goldman Sachs who funded the Cohn Jewish Student Center, as director of National Economic Council; Shulkin, a former undersecretary in the Obama administration and president of Beth Israel Medical Center in New York City, as secretary of Veterans Affairs, and so on.. Mnuchin and Cohn, the Goldman's golden boys, are the bankers of the West Wing's team surrounding the President and parts of the Jewish connexion with Jared and Ivanka.

To sum up, we have switched a 'black king' who was loving and kind for a 'white king' who is angry and mistrustful–for the dark side of the Force in a manner of speaking–to face other angry kings through the world, many of them being Muslims. The new king will wage the war and accelerate the climate change, but he will avoid the regional nuclear war which would bring a new Holocaust and pollute the global sky like 1,000 Chernobyl! He is the dark angel who announces the coming–in the near future–of the true Lord, who will be the master of time and of history, maybe Santorum–sanctum sanctorum–the Saint of Saints, thanks to the miraculous Z-machine and to its infinite source of energy.

We already drink from its well.

Éditeur : BoD-Books on Demand,
12/14 rond point des Champs Élysées, 75008 Paris, France
Impression : BoD-Books on Demand, Norderstedt, Allemagne
978-2-322-085095
Dépôt légal : octobre 2017